THE
Wedding

THE
Wedding

By Msgr. Richard Antall

Lambing Press | Pittsburgh

Lambing Press

Published in the United States by Lambing Press.

www.LambingPress.com

ISBN 978-0-9978215-8-1

Book design by Christina Aquilina

For Bobby, RIP

Chapter One

Holy Trinity Parish, Zachary, New Jersey

The first thing Fr. Bill Laughlin heard on the morning of June 24, 2001, was the noise his cellular phone made when it was on vibrate. The phone was on a nightstand next to his bed, so naturally he heard the buzz. He opened his eyes and said, "I bet it's him."

In a quick movement, the priest reached for the phone to see who was calling. It was Carl, just as he had thought. *I'll answer him a little later*, said the priest to himself. He recalled that a friend had said only a hospital should call before six o'clock in the morning. But this was Carl. *Poor bastard*, thought the priest, and then he said, "Sorry about that. I should have said *serviam*," this in quite a normal voice because he sometimes prayed aloud that way.

By the time he had got to the small bathroom that adjoined his bedroom (the latter adjoined a small living room which Laughlin always called his *"lebensraum"* because it was so small and because he enjoyed saying words in other languages, especially with historical references), Carl had called seven times, three from the telephone which was labelled "Carl" in Laughlin's contacts and four times on another line, also a cellular phone, which the priest had designated "Carl2."

"Hello, Carl," Laughlin said in a voice that he hoped

was not so weary.

"I can't believe it," said the other in a high-pitched voice with very rapid delivery.

"What can't you believe, Carl?" asked the priest. *I can't believe you are calling me at 6:05 a.m.*, he thought.

"I can't believe she cancelled," said Carl. Now he was talking in a normal voice, Fr. Bill noticed, but this thing that Carl did not believe had been the subject of at least thirty phone calls since the Friday before last.

"It is hard to believe, that you guys got so close to the actual date before she cancelled it. But, you know what our pastor said when he heard about it, 'One day you will consider it lucky that you did not carry this thing through.'"

"Thanks a lot, Father. Like I need that right now at six o'clock in the morning? You think that is going to help me sleep at night?"

"Did you have trouble sleeping last night?" asked the priest.

"No, not too bad. We had a ball game, which we lost to some old farts, but then we went to the sports bar. I had a few brews and then I went to bed."

And? thought Laughlin, but he did not say it.

"I just cannot believe that she decided to dump me for him. I mean, the guy is such a loser. I guess my mother is right, she wasn't worthy of me. But still, can you believe that she would pick George over me? When I sold him his car, I had to help him to ask questions. I should of screwed him on that car, but Mary wouldn't let me. He is such a wimp. I bet he wouldn't know what to do with a baseball mitt."

She wasn't picking a team for baseball, thought the priest, but he let the *apercu* pass by.

"I've got to get going," said Laughlin. "Maybe you could come in later." *What am I talking about? I don't want to see him again*, thought the priest. He was ready to step into the shower.

"Are you kidding me? I don't want to be caught dead at that place today."

That's a good idea, thought the priest. *Better than my own saying he could come by today.*

"Call me when you want to talk about it, but calm down, take it easy," he said to Carl. *Golden words*, he thought.

"Ok, I've got to go because we are going to play golf. On my wedding day, I know, it was to kill time. We had it planned and I said, sure, we are going to go through with it. What kind of a guy am I? We had it reserved. I will let you go, Father, thanks for calling."

"You called me," said Laughlin, but the other had hung up.

When he went down to breakfast, the Father Jako, the pastor, was at the table in what he always called the breakfast "nook." It was a corner of the breezeway between the rectory and the garage that some "illustrious predecessor" (another of the pastor's turns of phrase) of his had had enclosed and heated. There was a small table from which one looked out on a patio.

"Well how did you find the world when you woke up?" he asked Laughlin.

Pretty much the same as when I lost track of things, although brighter," said the priest. He knew that if he said this with a straight face, Fr. Jako would be amused. It was as he thought.

"You're awfully clever, too clever to be good, I am afraid," said the older priest.

"Is that the reason?" asked Laughlin.

"What do you have lined up today on your personal mission to save the world from itself?" asked the pastor.

"I am planning not to do the wedding that had been scheduled," he said.

"Oh, that is still on your mind."

"The groom not-to-be called me at six this morning."

"For the love of Pete. You get too involved with these people. You're not helping anyone that way, least of all yourself, but not them either. Was he trying to cry on your shoulder?"

"Not exactly. He just said that he could *not* believe what happened."

"Well, he better start. The poor bastard. Was he really broke up about it?"

"Yes and no. He was going out to do eighteen holes of golf."

"Oh no. And so he calls you at six in the morning to tell you that?"

"I guess so," he said. "I invited him to come over later, but he said no."

"Thanks be to God he has a little more sense than you. You cannot go on like this. No wedding, the thing is over. You always go too far. Pius XI talked about the heresy of activism. Think about that. No one can carry these bleeding idiots around all the time. Remember what Moses's father-in-law told him in the desert. Cut the umbilical cord, or whatever, let them sink or swim according to their own drummer. Get the hell out of their lives."

Nice collection of metaphors, Louis Bertrand, Laughlin said to himself. That was Father Jako's baptismal name, Louis Bertrand. His mother had been a cook at a Dominican parish and one of the priests had convinced her to name her son after one of their saints. The younger priest was looking at him, and thought, *he is tired. Almost everything he says has the style of a parting shot. Maybe he really is on his way out, like the bishop had said.* He wondered if Jako knew the bishop was betting he would retire soon for health reasons. The way the bishop talked about the pastor at a priests' gathering had sounded strange to Laughlin, as if Jako's retirement would be a relief to him.

Jako stood up but leaned forward with his hands on the back of a chair. The older priest was tall, but his corpulence no longer gave the impression of strength that it perhaps had in years before. The center of gravity of his body was in his gut between the heavy hips, one of which had an implanted artificial socket. Jako had said, "I am the bionic priest." But when he walked now-- somewhat carefully because he must have taken a few spills, which, of course, he never admitted-- he gave the impression of a concerted effort, not of ease. His white hair, straight, and very full was a little longer than one might expect for a man his age. The glasses gave his face the look of an aviator from the beginnings of flight. He squinted through them now at Laughlin with his baby blues.

"Cat got your tongue?" said his pastor.

The older priest's light blue eyes met the younger's dark blue eyes. Laughlin smiled and this provoked a kind of movement of muscles on the face of the older priest that the younger priest called a "snigger" to the delight of one of his friends we will meet very soon. Laughlin was reminded that Jako had also had a mild stroke.

That and the diabetes and the hip thing made for a rather thick medical chart. His diabetes was from drinking the water at certain Buddhist shrines in the Far East on a grand tour Jako had taken with a nephew. At least that was Jako's hypothesis of how he got "sugar in the blood". He must have thought it was some kind of divine punishment for idolatry.

"No, I'm just thinking about what you said. I should not have invited him to stop by today."

"The light bulb has been turned on," said Father Jako.

Then Laughlin's phone went off again.

"Here he is, on his way over. You better finish your cereal."

But it was not Carl who was calling. It was his bride-not-to-be.

"Hello, Father, I am sorry to call you so early. It's just. It's just."

"I know this must be a tough day for you, Mary," Laughlin said. He saw that Jako had figured out who the caller was, and was amused.

"For crying out loud, I don't know if this is a soap opera or a sit com," said Jako to the air.

"Mary, are you there?" She had hung up.

"Well, that makes two of them," said Jako. "Don't tell me she changed her mind."

"No, I don't think so. She feels sorry for Carl. She told me once, 'He is an egomaniac jerk who thinks he is the center of the universe but I still feel bad for putting him through this.'"

"A tough girl with a heart of gold. You have a real gift for attracting people," said Jako.

"It is not an easy situation. Her parents were upset."

"Well, sure, they probably lost the deposit on the hall," said Jako.

"I don't think it was *just* that," said Laughlin, but he was laughing. *Leave it to Jako to read the situation from an economic perspective.*

At this point Peter Aquino came into kitchen. He looked into the breakfast nook.

"Well, greetings, *Frater*," said Jako.

"Greetings," said the priest with a pronounced accent. He was from the Philippines.

"Hello Peter," said Laughlin.

The late arrival began to fuss about the kitchen, taking bowls and boxes out of cupboards and using the microwave to heat water.

"I wonder what is on the menu today," said Jako.

"Uh, maybe oatmeal?" said Laughlin.

"You mock me, but I have no problems with digestion,"

said a voice from around the corner in the kitchen.

Indigestion was a human suffering that dominated the mind of Fr. Aquino. *Perhaps he had suffered some chronic problem when he was studying in Pamplona, in New Haven, or in Washington,* thought Laughlin, looking at the wizened priest, who appeared in the doorway. Some of the altar boys called Yoda. Although he was Filipino, his features were Chinese. His age, "according to what he let on" as Jako put it, was seventy, but he could easily have been older. It was not that he was not active, because he was considerably more agile physically than Jako, who was almost the same age, but the wrinkles on his face and the inscrutable expression in his eyes made him seem like some species from another planet.

He sat down opposite to Laughlin with his bowl of oatmeal, the only thing he would eat for breakfast.

"You've got wedding today?" he asked Laughlin.

"There you go, that is the sixty-four-thousand-dollar question," said Jako, who had remained standing a few feet away from the table.

"I thought you had wedding today," said Father Peter. He had characteristically ignored the pastor, with whom he had worked the last ten years of his life.

"It was called off," said Laughlin.

"Called off," said Peter, "Today?"

"Actually, last week. The invitations were out already."

"Tell him the bride and groom are still calling you." Jako liked to give news.

"Actually, both are pretty broke up about it," said Laughlin.

"No marriage? Schedule says you have marriage." said Father Peter.

The man knew five languages, and yet had trouble with English. He had studied at Yale, and even given a course there, but he had such trouble with endings. Laughlin wondered if the same problems occurred for Peter in Italian, Spanish and French, his other languages. Maybe Tagalog did not modify endings that much.

"I'm sorry, I forgot to change it on the board," said Laughlin. *Peter lives by the schedule.*

"What happened?" asked Peter.

"Well the girl had this friend."

"I must go," interrupted Jako.

He was going out to get the paper and his breakfast dessert, which he bought at a local bakery. Sometimes he came home with a bag of lady locks and took them straight to his room.

"Good bye," said Father Peter, *without remorse* and without even looking up from his oatmeal. The "without remorse" was a phrase Jako used to describe his fellow priest, as in, "He would walk over my dead body without remorse if one of his Filipino ladies was at the door." This was supposedly based on a spill Jako had taken on the stairs. He was not yet completely upright when Aquino rushed by to answer the door, almost knocking him down again. That was before Jako started using the elevator.

"I'll do the 4:30 p.m. because I have to give the financial report and the Knights are coming." Jako often had this sort of false *denouement*. It was not always over when it seemed it was over.

"The Knight of Columbus?" asked the Filipino priest.

"Why do you ask?"

"Who take care of bingo?" asked Father Peter.

"Some second-stringers. There is some kind of dinner for the Knights. Giving someone another award."

"Humph." The Filipino priest was given to such Delphic utterances. Laughlin noticed that Jako had not even blinked an eye.

The doorbell rang.

"Who could this be?" asked Jako, alarmed.

The door opened of itself and Marilu, the woman who served as volunteer sacristan walked in.

"Why did you ring the doorbell if you had the key?" asked Jako.

"Well, Father, I wanted to make sure you were decent."

She was a heavy woman, called big-boned by those who liked her, who were many. She had a wide, pleasant face, a sarcastic sense of humor and a lilting laugh. Laughlin heard, however, that she had had a hard life with her husband. The latter was a little man with a mean expression on his face. An incongruous couple: you would never put the two together if you were not told to do so. Laughlin had heard two women talking about him once and one had said, "He used to be even worse."

"He never is decent," said Father Peter over his oatmeal, and smiled.

"Alright, that is enough. I will do the 4:30. Which of you wants the 6 p.m.?"

"I can do it," said Laughlin.

"No, I do it. You have *Catecumenos*, tonight" said Peter.

That was something Laughlin had forgotten. It was his turn to do the Mass with the Neo-Catechumens. *Peter always remembers the schedule, because he has so little else to remember. Not the surprises that come my way,* exempla gratia: *the wedding that will not happen.*

"What is that?" asked Jako.

"Neo Cats," said Laughlin.

"May Allah be praised," said Jako.

"I am here about the wedding, Father," said Marilu.

"There is no wedding," barked Jako.

"I know that, but shouldn't we put up a sign or something? I think that many of the invited guests do not know that it was called off."

Marilu had been the first on the staff to know about the wedding cancellation, because she handled both rehearsals and the setup of the church.

"I guess I'll put something up," said Laughlin.

"I got a sign; I just wanted to have permission to put it up."

"Farewell," said Jako.

Marilu was looking expectantly at Laughlin.

"Well?" she said.

"What does the sign say?"

"I have two versions, one says, 'Horvath-Sand wedding cancelled' and the other 'Horvath-Sand wedding postponed.'"

"We will go with the first one," said Laughlin.

There would be a million questions to answer if we put up the second sign, he thought. *There would be people knocking on the door. And only Carl apparently thought it might be only a postponement.*

"I'm going out for lunch with a friend," Laughlin said.

No one acknowledged this piece of information. Maybe they expected him to say who the friend was, he thought.

"I'm going to see a nun in the hospital. Sister Margarita. She worked at my deacon parish, Saints. Philip and James. Ronald Avery is coming and we're going to see her and then lunch," he said.

This sparked interest. Father Peter looked up from his bowl, which was nearly empty. And Marilu smiled.

"Tell Ronald Avery I sent my best. That boy is crazy. You aren't going to take him to the hospital to see the nunny bunny are you?" Marilu was obviously amused. She had heard Ronald call Sister Margarita "nunny bunny" once and thought it was the height of humor.

"I think so," said Laughlin.

"He's bound to create a stir," said Marilu. Her Southern accent made everything she said sound funnier.

"I hope not. But if he makes Sor Margarita laugh, it will

be worth it."

Father Laughlin didn't want to see the nun by himself. He was afraid that she would get too emotional, although he knew she might resent sharing a visit with Ron.

"What do we tell people who come here?" Aquino had thought of something unpleasant, judging by the sour look on his face.

"What do you mean, Father?" asked Marilu.

"People come to door. They are asking, 'what the heck happened?' What should I say?"

"You say you don't know," said Marilu patiently.

On a certain level, nobody really knows, thought Laughlin.

Chapter Two

A little later, Laughlin went to the chapel to get the Holy Communion to take to the hospital for Margarita. Fr. Peter was there doing his spiritual reading. It looked like he was reading Seneca again. It was an old book the priest had picked up at a second hand bookshop, copyright 1882, from an edition made by a Sir Roger L'Estrange, an English Cavalier during the Civil War in Britain. The book was an "Abstract" of the pagan philosopher's work, a kind of digest that eliminated everything but his moral teaching. Seneca was an unusual choice for spiritual reading, but Laughlin had picked the book more than once and been impressed. He also loved the author's surname.

Father Peter had underlined various passages. One part said something like, "It is a dangerous office to give good advice to intemperate princes." That was certainly the story of Seneca's life, since he was a councillor to Nero. Laughlin had wondered whether it was something Father Peter felt about himself. Although the Filipino was very circumspect, it was said that Peter had been close to President Marcos at some point in the dictator's political career.

The priest had taught at the University of St. Thomas and eventually become a critic of Marcos within academic and ecclesiastical circles. Then the priest had had to flee. Actually, he had been visiting friends in America when he received a call warning him not to return to Manila. The woman who had told Laughlin this—and with the Filipinos it was usually a woman who would tell you something like this-- had claimed that Father Peter was a close relative to Corazon Aquino's husband, the one Marcos had assassinated.

"Not so close, yes, cousins, but I'm related to Imelda, also," was the only thing that Father Peter had said when Laughlin asked him.

Or maybe the intemperate prince was Jako. Many people believed, and this included the other priests in the neighborhood, that Peter Aquino was Jako's conscience. "He won't go as far as he might if he didn't have the Chink with him over there," said one of the presbyters. "The little guy keeps Jako in line." This sort of enigmatic oracle was the table talk of the deanery.

Greatness, said Seneca, was always something composed and quiet. "The boldest tongues have the faintest hearts," was another phrase Laughlin remembered being underlined in the book. Father Peter did not have a faint heart. From being an intellectual that a dictator had reason to be preoccupied about, the priest had become what he was today, a "senior associate pastor" in a small town in New Jersey. He himself joked about being a "Mass priest, like in the Middle Ages, when some were ordained only to pray for dead." This brilliant man, with his sometimes difficult English, serving in an aging parish in the city of Zachary, New Jersey, was an example to the younger priest. In humiliation, there is the possibility of nobility.

Laughlin opened the tabernacle and took out a host, which he laid on the open pyx, which he then closed and wrapped in the leather pouch that Mrs. Calvey had given him—a widow who had had an awful time of grief. He thought of her each time he carried the Eucharist because the case had her name on it, "given in gratitude by." Laughlin looked at Fr. Peter as he walked out of the chapel. The priest had his eyes closed and his face looked like a character out of Fu Manchu. The reason the name came to Laughlin was because Father Jako, in some moods, would call him that, too. He also said he was "the inscrutable Asiatic." It was not always clear when the pastor was kidding, even when he provided himself with his own laugh track.

He was almost out of the chapel when his phone went off again. He rushed out of the chapel to answer.

"Yes," he said.

"William, I am coming, so don't worry about me. Just got a late start."

"How unusual for you, Ronald Avery."

"Don't be smart. Remember you have to walk a mile in another man's moccasins."

"I wouldn't dare try yours on. Remember the *fungus amongus* scare at Seton."

Ron laughed, "I can't say I blame you there."

"Maybe I should go to the hospital first, then," he said. *That would mean being alone with the nun.*

"I told you I am on my way, Child, don't be in such a huffy mood."

"I am not in a huffy mood, just have work to do. What does 'on my way' mean, anyway? That you have the keys to your car in your hand? That you are walking down the steps to go out right now? Or that you are still in your pyjamas?"

"Keys in the hand, hear them jingle."

"You're at a McDonald's."

"William, you have an unearthly keen sense of hearing. I can't believe you. They could put you on television or something, 'the psychic priest.' I will be there in ten minutes. I am on the outskirts of the village."

He rang off, as they said in British novels, thought Laughlin. It was one of his trademark phrases. He had spent a great deal of time in college seminary finding or inventing phrases to punctuate reality. "Takes the edge off harsh reality," that was another of his phrases and a good understanding of why he said them. The priest had always wanted to string them all together in a little book, but that ambition stayed unfulfilled.

Now he had a few minutes on his hands. He had already said his office, rather too hurriedly, as usual. Sometimes he prayed the psalms of the breviary with a spirit of reflection but mostly he read them. At a retreat once, an older priest had shocked him by saying that he "wasn't a great fan of Hebrew poetry." That meant that the other priest did not like to say the prayers that were called the "Office." Laughlin would not ever say what the other had said, but wondered sometimes whether it was not true of himself, also. Perhaps because the psalms and canticles were so familiar to him, he was seldom arrested by a beautiful expression. *Maybe much was lost in the translation of Hebrew poetry,* he thought.

He had the Eucharist in the pyx hanging around his neck, and so he felt uncomfortable walking around the house. Although he was not pious enough to pray constantly to the Lord he believed present in the wafer of bread in the little leather case, nevertheless, he felt embarrassed that he was not more devout. Father Peter once saw him wearing the pouch, with the pyx without the Eucharist and almost genuflected. He had forgotten to take it off his neck after giving someone communion and had met the other priest on the stairs. "No, Father Peter, He's not here--it's empty," he had said.

Now he went to his room. He looked at his lounge chair and saw his copy of *American Pastoral*. Carrying the Eucharist and looking at the book made him blush. He had read the novel two times. The first time, he had left it by accident in the living room of the rectory and Father

Aquino had picked it up.

The priest had waited until the pastor was away for lunch to bring up the topic.

"Reading Philip Roth?"

"Yes, he is an amazing author."

"Amazing but perverse. This book about the girl and the bombing. Her father kiss her. Theme of incest. Also very American Jewish-- everything connected to sex. Also hostility to Catholics."

"But it is much more than that. It's about America and family and New Jersey. The Dwyers, the family of the wife, are from Elizabeth. The father of the main character is anti-Catholic, but it is a caricature. I can't believe Roth was that anti-Catholic. He makes the grandfather Levov into a monster."

"Be careful what you read. Like what you eat. You become it. Nice to have intellectual pursuits, but always spiritual reading, always Bible."

Laughlin had not asked how Father Peter knew so much about the book. It was the second time around before he saw how important incest was to the theme of *American Pastoral*. But reading Roth on Elizabeth, New Jersey, was like sharing a perspective on his life not so very far away from Elizabeth that others around him seemed to have missed.

A spiritual reading book some parishioners had given him was lying in the debris on his desk. He picked it up gingerly and found the place where he had left off. Several days had passed and he had not looked at it. "Your prayer life lacks a little *je ne sais quoi*," he said to himself. That was a tag from a professor in the seminary. He read the first paragraph that caught his eye:

> *He is a strange and a lonely man. This is*
> *inevitable since he is situated on the boundary*

> *between both those worlds. He is in the world*
> *and yet he belongs to another world which he*
> *has not yet entered. Consequently "he is the*
> *everlasting outsider who is supposed to be not*
> *of this world, a man who has been removed from*
> *the purely human sphere, one whom men think*
> *of as alien and peculiar. He is a being signed*
> *and separate, a man who stands at the margin*
> *of life, and who is yet continually drawn to its*
> *center."*

"There's a real pick-you-up kind of thought, the priest as *Steppenwolf*," Laughlin said to himself, and then was shocked to realize that he was speaking aloud. His cell phone was humming again. It was Mary.

There I was at the border of the skies and then she pulls me back to the goofy earth.

"Father," Mary's voice had a special tone of pleading when she said the word, "I'm sorry my phone went dead when I was talking to you. It lost its charge, like everything else in my life. I've got it on the charger now. What I want to know is, has Carl called you?"

"Just twice, but we talked very briefly."

"Oh God, he is so crazy. I am surprised it was only twice." She talked like that Sandy Dennis character in *The Out of Towners* (a favorite movie of his mother); every sentence began like a prayer.

"I think he will be ok. He was going to go golfing."

"Oh God. Golfing! Nothing more important than golf. My brother was invited, originally. Well, I guess that is ok. If he went out with the guys, then he probably won't follow through with the threat."

Laughlin was silent, expecting to be told what the threat entailed. However, Mary had paused.

"Threat?" he said.

"He said that he was going to run over George with his car." The priest thought, *Shouldn't it be, "run George over"?*

"When did he say that? Recently?"

"He sent me an e-mail last night."

"He can't be serious."

"You don't know how macho he is. Meanwhile, George is not...George is not a fighter."

Meanwhile George is not a fighter? Nevertheless, he won the battle, thought Laughlin.

"Father Laughlin?" the voice had asked. "Yes," he had answered.

"I want to ask you a question. Do you think somebody should get married to a person just because she doesn't want to hurt their feelings?"

Their feelings. It was a rather typical Midwestern construction, the substitution of the possessive plural form for the singular. Laughlin himself made the mistake frequently, and George was from Ohio, too. The question was about not hurting the feelings of someone, singular.

"Why are you asking me this?" Laughlin had responded. It was past eleven o'clock, he had the six o'clock Mass the next morning and he was someone who needed his sleep.

"Because you are supposed to do the wedding." The voice sounded bored, or impatient with the priest's stupidity.

How was he supposed to know the general question was about the Sand-- Horvath wedding?

"Which wedding?" he had several weddings planned for that summer.

"You will find out, I hope," said the voice, male, maybe

in his late twenties, a familiar kind of tone.

"Wait a minute," said the priest. But the caller had not waited. "Well, I never heard of that one," Laughlin had said to himself. That was another line from the seminary, one an especially peculiar Greek teacher had used with frequency.

Ronny had called immediately after this strange conversation. Was it a joke, then? "Could Ronny disguise his voice that well?" Laughlin had wondered. It had taken him awhile to conclude that the call was not a prank.

But Mary was still on the phone during this reverie of thought. "Father, George would like to meet you again."

You meet someone once, and then you "see" them again. Unless you are speaking about meeting "with" someone. That was Laughlin's take on the situation. He was unconscious that he was making the usual mistake about the plural pronoun, seeing "them."

"What is he doing?" asked the priest.

It was a ridiculous question. What is he doing? Like, is he out mowing the lawn? Did he go golfing? Had he been invited? One of the stranger aspects of the case was that the two men, Carl and George, had known each other. He was "one of her friends from work." She had brought George along with her to Carl's baseball games so she didn't have to sit alone in the stands— she didn't like the teammates' girlfriends-- and even to the bar where the whole gang, would usually go afterwards. How had she introduced him? "This is George; he is falling in love with me"?

"Right now, he is sleeping. We were up late talking last night. My parents are going to kill me, because I stayed here at George's house. First, we were cleaning, and then we watched *Casablanca.* Then Joyce came over to talk. She is --I mean was—one of my bridesmaids. She was telling us about this old movie, *The Graduate*, which she said was sort of like what we did or what we were going through—a ruined wedding. George tried to download it on the computer, but he couldn't. I tell you, Father, I, we, didn't do anything wrong. George slept on the couch. "

He remembered Joyce. She had come as a special emissary from Mary to tell him that the mysterious man on the phone was not lying but that the decision to call off the marriage had not yet been made but was bound to come down any day. Joyce had not seemed terribly upset about it. In fact, she had been a little thrilled with the idea of being the bearer of gossip. Was she, he had wondered, secretly pleased with the breakup?

Or maybe the drama thrilled her.

She had laughed and said, "What is this, like torn between two lovers?"

Or perhaps, even when she was sighing "poor Baby" about her friend Mary, who was "supposingly"—her word--in love with both men Joyce had her eye on Carl.

She had praised him. He remembered her saying especially that he was manlier than George, and had offered a better life to Mary.

Mary was still chattering away.

"First, Joyce was going to stay, too. She would have stayed with me. Then she remembered that she had a baby shower to go to on Sunday, and she wanted to look her best. I had got these coupons, and they included nails with the hair. But it had to be today early in the morning because supposedly we were going to have the wedding. It was now or never, or pay for it all on her own. So she thought she might as well. She didn't want to waste the money I had paid for it."

Where is this going? Laughlin felt like he was stranded.

"Then it was so late, and I did not look forward to waking up in my house, where everyone is *trying* so hard not to throw into my face that I have disgraced the whole family, but it is so obvious they cannot understand. Except my brother Ray, of course. He's all right about everything, because he hated Carl from day one. But that is another story."

And which story is this?

"I am taking up a lot of your time, Father, I am sorry. I just want the afternoon to come. I wish that I could be so busy between eleven and twelve that I would not even think about how I screwed up."

"You know what I told you about that. When something is past, we have to move on. It had to happen and now it's over. What we can't avoid, we have to accept."

"What cannot be eschewed must be embraced," as Shakespeare would have it. I don't say that to you because I don't want to be pretentious. I wish I thought of Scripture quotes as fast as I can poetry sometimes.

"I know Father. You are such a consolation. George is out of it today. In the morning he said that he felt like we were living some kind of movie and he was afraid I would end up going to the church anyway, and you would marry Carl and me with the janitor and the sacristan lady as the only witnesses, and he wouldn't see me again. Men are such babies sometimes--- I mean it in a nice way. So simple or something."

"Thank you," said Laughlin.

"Oh yeah, I'm sorry. I forgot you are one of them, too. Ha ha. That's good. I needed that today."

"Helllloooo," Laughlin heard from the stairwell below.

"Just a second, Mary," he said. "Ron, I am up here, come on up."

I trust your feminine intuition will enable you to sense our conversation is reaching a conclusion.

"You're busy, Father, I'm sorry. I'll call you later. I think maybe George will need to see you today. He's all tied up in emotional knots. I mean, I am traumatized, but he is a basket case."

"Ok, Mary, call me later." *There you go again. Today? So that was the "meet" she had meant he wanted to "meet with" me again. As in today?*

Now Ron was in the room, as large as life. Or maybe a little larger than he used to be, he was getting fat since he hung up his cassock.

Chapter Three

*"*Ronny, my boy, you've grown," said Laughlin.

"Get out of here," said the other, "I am losing weight."

"I think it's finding you again, somehow," said the priest, "You must be doing well or at least eating well in the world. The dry cleaning business must be going ok."

"It is not. Well, it's ok. People are such snots sometimes, though."

"You used to say that when you were in the parish."

"That was at St. Jude's. You must not talk to me about St. Jude's, William. If you don't walk the walk, you cannot talk the talk."

Laughlin looked at his visitor. He was dressed in tan slacks, which were slipping down from his belly, which did this overhang number on them. Ron wore a shirt that was a variety of colors, in a kind of swirling pattern that seemed to work ok, but that was probably "ethnic", the code word the two used. Laughlin would not have looked good in that shirt, although he probably had worn similar ones in the seventies. That was when all kind of things were allowed, like those awful shoes with the big heels.

"Why are you looking at me? Have you never seen a handsome man of color before?"

"Sure, Sidney Poitier. He was in *The Lilies of the Field*. 'A-men, a-men, a-men, etc.'" he was singing this off key to the delight of his friend. "Remember how much Schmidt liked that amen."

"Oh, Fr. Schmidt. What ever happened to him?"

"He went to live in the monastery and then he died. I invited you to go to his funeral to sing *Amazing Grace* but you were too busy."

"You are terrible William. I really was too busy."

"Yeah, you were probably planning your next trip to Rome."

"I went twice. You never wanted to go."

"Didn't have the money."

"Money was not the issue. I didn't have money either."

"But you had that credit card."

He wondered if this was going too far, but Ron did not look upset. He was looking at the books Laughlin had laying around the sitting room. *The Cousins' War* by Kevin Phillips was on the top of a pile of magazines and books on a coffee table. Ron was paging through it with interest.

"Ronny, I am beginning to see gray twirls in your 'fro."

"I do not have a fro, bro. Leave me alone, I am looking at this book. You know I love history. And neither do I have gray hair. God, you want to make me feel old or something?"

"Are you talking to me or are you praying?"

"What are you saying to me?"

"I heard you say, 'God'. I thought you might be praying."

"Don't take the Lord's name in vain."

"Like you did. Remember when you couldn't name the Ten Commandments in Buckley's class?"

"I could name them. You are such an exaggerator, William. Didn't your mother teach you not to lie?"

"Which commandment is that?"

"The seventh."

"Ron! The eighth."

"I was just kidding. I know the Ten Commandments."

"Once you gave them like the Baptists do. You got the numbers mixed up."

"Just shut your mouth. Now, let me just sit down."

"No, we have got to go to the hospital to see someone."

"I just got here."

"From Trenton?"

"Yes, from Trenton."

"How come I smell McDonald's on your breath?"

"You do not smell McDonald's on my breath. You must be delirious. Who is in the hospital?"

"Sor Margarita."

"I'm sorry, who?"

"Sor Margarita."

"Am I supposed to know this Mrs. Sor?"

"Sor, as you will recall, is short for the Latin, *soror*, sister. She is the nun who went with the group to the Holy Land."

"The Spanish one? The one that was in love with you?"

"Yes, not from Spain, but Mexico. Yeah, for you, the Spanish one."

"Is she sick?"

"No, she is in the maternity section."

"Maternity? Isn't she a nun no more?"

"*Reductio ad absurdum.* Of course she is sick if she is in the hospital. You asked 'Is she sick?' Why else would she be in the hospital?"

"Well, maybe she just bore you a love-child. She had such a crush on you. The poor woman. I don't know what she could have seen in you."

The two were laughing and their voices had increased in volume during the conversation. As a result, they didn't hear the steps in the hallway. Then, suddenly—a word not much used for the movements of a man of his girth, Fr. Louis Bertrand Jako was standing in the doorway.

"There goes the neighborhood," he said and gave his

crooked smile.

"There goes the neighborhood," Ron laughed, "That's right; it just took a step up."

Ron never minds Jako's racial slurs, Laughlin thought.

"A step up. Huh! How are you, Ronald?"

It was funny how the pastor joked around with Ron because he was not exactly a bleeding heart on racial issues. He used to recount how he had suffered during the riots in Trenton when he had been stationed at a small ethnic parish. Two things came to Laughlin's mind. One was the annual stewardship sermon in which the pastor spoke about contribution to the Church. Jako was prone to use words that one only found now in books: "Please, people, don't be niggardly in your collection envelope." Laughlin had wished that he had that on tape. The other thing was the pastor's obsession with the detective from the O.J. Simpson case, the one who used the "n" word and then wrote a book about some Kennedy hanger-on who might have killed a girl. Jako could not get over the not guilty decision for O.J.

"I am thriving, Father, thank you for asking."

Laughlin wondered whether Father Jako had any idea of the depth of irony that could invest itself in this supposed gratitude.

"Thriving eh? Why didn't you bring me any movies?"

Videos were a kind of passion for Jako. He must have watched three to five a week, sometimes more. And none of them worthwhile movies, at least in Laughlin's eyes. The pastor liked cowboy movies, and action flicks.

"Ronny has gone into another business," Laughlin said.

"What, did the movie rental thing go belly up?"

Jako had a curiosity for economic detail and a lack of discretion that would embarrass a reporter for *The National Enquirer.*

"He has gone into dry cleaning," he said.

"Dry cleaning? In Trenton?"

"Fresh as a flower within the hour," said Laughlin.

"Are you kidding me, same day service?"

"Theoretically, but most people opt for the normal two-day or three-day service," Ron lied.

Laughlin knew, because he had visited the place, that the fresh-as-a-flower bit was a joke. Besides, Ron had to send the clothes out to another cleaner, because he did not have the machines to do the cleaning.

"Is that going better than the videos? A lot of dry cleaning in Trenton?" Jako very deliberately looked over at Laughlin.

What was that look supposed to mean? Did he know that many customers never reclaimed their clothing?

"It's going well, everything takes time to build in small business administration," said Ronald.

"Well, have a nice lunch or whatever you are going to do," said Jako, "Your pal knows that you had the wedding of the year today, I suppose."

Ron was quick to look at Laughlin to try to understand.

"A wedding was cancelled," he said. Then Laughlin addressed Jako, "The almost-bride also called. The almost-groom threatened to run over the actual boyfriend."

"You certainly have a gift," said Jako. He looked at Ronald. "Your man really has some loonies among his friends and admirers."

"Don't I know it," said Ronald.

Laughlin noticed the pastor carried a bakery bag in his hand as he shuffled down the hallway.

"I thought we were going to the hospital," said Ron.

"We are, then lunch. There is a Cuban place I want to take you."

"Who cancels a wedding?"

Non sequitur, but typical, thought Laughlin.

"A girl who finds out she is really in love with another man."

"Really. How wo-mantic."

"Both bride and groom have called me more than once today."

"Who was she in love with?" said Ron. "Did they just cancel today?"

He has a good bit of Schadenfreude in him. In that, he and Jako are a match.

"No, it was cancelled last week. The bride got involved with another man."

"Well, that is interesting. Did the groom find out just in time?"

"Actually, he tried to talk her out of the 'infatuation,' as he called it. One of his arguments was that they would lose the money spent on their planned honeymoon. He said they should go and maybe she would stay with him. She would not hear of it. There is more to the story, though, it is pretty complicated."

Jako burst into laughter. Laughlin had not noticed that the man had retraced his steps and was in the doorway of his suite.

"Complicated, no kidding," he said in his nasal voice. "Your buddy attracts some of the weirdest cases, I tell you."

"Oh, you're not telling me nothing I didn't know!"

Ron was laughing.

He doesn't know Jako has him in the same category: "Weird cases for a hundred, please."

Jako had decided that his second Parthian shot was the last of the day and turned to go down the hall.

"Stewards of the mysteries of God." The old bucko has to fight to keep his head above water, physically, at least, who knows spiritually? And he never tires of his jokes, which are not all that funny. I could really say what St. Peter lied about, "I do not know the man," even though I live in the same house. Our

conversations were always sarcastic. The banter is like something out of Samuel Becket—theatre of the absurd, a writer Jako has never read. Still, the old guy was no doubt trying to be nice or he would not have stopped to talk to Ronny. Something about Ronny fascinated him, or was it that I could have such a friend and appear "normal" to Jako?

They fell silent and could hear Jako unlocking his door.

"What's he got in his room that he had double locks on it?"

"Probably the wad of cash he keeps as his expense account, so-called petty cash," Bill said, "Let's go."

"He's so funny, William. You just don't appreciate his humor."

"You're probably right. I think I will like him more at a distance. Like when I am retired and writing my memoirs."

"What are you going to write about me?"

"Depends on how you behave," he said.

"You are my friend, William," Ronald Avery, Jr., was suddenly very serious.

"Of course," said Laughlin.

"And friends have unconditional love," said Ron.

"Pardon me?"

"You know what I said."

"I thought you said unconditional love, but that is a phrase that can be applied to Our Lord but not to anybody else."

"You don't love me unconditionally?"

"What are you talking about? Let's go, the nun is waiting."

"*She* loves you unconditionally."

"I don't think so, because she made so many conditions. The poor thing is dying, though. I really feel bad about it. I disappointed her."

"By not falling in love with her? Did you tell her she wasn't your type? That you can only really love your books?"

"Where is that coming from? *Vámonos*, we've got to go to the hospital."

"Maybe I'll just stay here and watch TV 'till you come back."

"No way, get up." Ron was already sitting down on the small couch.

"William, I need to rest from my journey, and I haven't seen television for two weeks. My brain cells are craving visual stimulation."

"Let's go."

"William, you don't listen very well. Boy, your momma did not raise you right. Spare the rod and spoil the child."

"I thought it was an insult to say boy to a man," Laughlin said as he grabbed Ronald's arm to lift him up.

"Not to you, you are white, remember that, Child."

"My conditional love says we have to get to the car. You can watch TV at home."

"No, the dumb store came and took my TV back."

"Oops, let's start walking. Step by step, you're going to make it. 'Heidi, you can walk!'"

"William, you are a strange child," said Ron, but he was laughing.

"Thank you. That will help my wounded self-image tremendously."

On the stairs they met Fr. Peter, who greeted Ron fondly.

They all like him so much, thought Laughlin. *Or are they friendly with him to show friendship to me? They are not so friendly and smiling with me, maybe it's easier for them to be like that with Ron.*

They were in the car, and Laughlin had put the key in the ignition when Ron turned to him.

"Is your pastor a bigot?" he asked.

Laughlin turned to his friend and saw that he was

smiling.

"Is this the face of a bigot?" Laughlin and Ron had a riff on an old impression of George Wallace, the "segregation-forever" governor.

"Probably, and unaccountably, he nevertheless seems to like you," he said.

"Probably and unaccountably, William, you watch too much of that William F. Buckley show. What's the 'F' for anyway?"

"I'll ask him next time I lunch with him."

Chapter Four

It was both better and worse than Laughlin thought it would be. Better because she was so happy to receive Holy Communion and then because Sister Margarita had relaxed and joked around. She accepted the visit with Ron and her criticism about Laughlin's ignoring her was said in a humorous way. It was worse because she was evidently going down physically. After a few minutes, he couldn't understand what she was saying. She had never been easy to understand, both because of the accent and because she used to swallow her words. Now, the weakness had made her practically incomprehensible.

Of course Ron was no help at all in that aspect. *I should have known he would complicate things.* Mr. Avery understood her less than Laughlin. Even worse he asked his friend to clarify what Sister was saying when the former had no idea of what had been said.

She had joked from the first thing.

"Who is that?" she had said and pointed to Laughlin.

"She's asking you who I am because I haven't been to see her in a week."

"He is terrible, Sister," said Ron, "He has this amnesia about friends."

"Amnesia?" Laughlin said.

"How are you?' said Sister, looking at Laughlin. Then to Ron, "Where have you been?"

Ron's face registered he didn't understand a word of what she said.

"Ronny, she is asking where you've been. Well, today, Sor Margarita, he is an entrepreneur and dry-cleaning magnate. We were classmates, so I am pleased he still remembers me. You met him once, at least. He was with me once at a reunion of the Holy Land Pilgrimage Group."

She nodded and smiled, but looked at Laughlin seriously. He knew that she had remembered now that Ron was the friend who had left the priesthood. As a religious, she saw that as a tremendous tragedy.

"*Donde has estado?*" she asked Laughlin. She was a little clearer in Spanish.

"Still working. The parish is really busy. Both of the other priests are not young. I had a funny thing happen today. Well, not really funny, just different. There was a couple that was going to get married today and they decided not to, or really she decided not to get married because she was really in love with another man---this guy from work."

He had run on like that, partly because he preferred monolog to trying to decipher what Sister had to say. Her eyes had opened wide at his story. *People think runaway brides are interesting.*

She murmured something but he hadn't the slightest idea of what she said.

"What did she say?" asked Ron.

"She asked me how your drying cleaning business was going," he said.

"It's going alright, Sister, thank you for asking. I am not making much money, but I am keeping at keeping at it, you know."

Her brows bunched up about that.

"Tell her in Spanish that I am doing ok," Ron said.

"I spik inglish," the nun said.,

"What did she say?" asked Ron.

"She wants to know how you are really. Why you haven't been around?"

"Doesn't she know I have left?" asked Ron.

"She knows everything, and then some," said Laughlin. He winked at Sister and saw that she was in on the joke. Again she murmured something.

"Translate, what is she saying now?"

You idiot, Ronny, I am going to whup you when we get out of the hospital.

"She is saying that she is praying for you."

Sister shook her head.

"I mean that she is not praying for you."

She shook her head again.

"*Mentira*," she whispered, at least that is what he made out.

Then she pointed to Ron and folded her hands, and then gestured to him.

"Oh, she thinks you should be praying."

"Tell her I am praying, especially the week the rent is due. Yep, I pray a lot."

Sister Margarita shook her head, but she was smiling.

Laughlin said a prayer, holding her hand when he did so. She didn't want to let go. Ron noticed that immediately, and tears came to his eyes. This affected Laughlin, who felt his throat tighten.

"Well, we better be going. Ronny drove up from Trenton and is hungry, although I know he stopped at a McDonald's. He had an accident, by the way. He is driving a rental."

"How do you know that, William?"

"Because you owned a car last time I knew and would not drive a rental if it cost you extra. I deduced you had an accident."

"It wasn't my fault."

Margarita was following all this closely.

As if she should care about all this when she is at the end of the line. You'd think that some of her family would come to visit her at this moment, so that I don't feel so guilty not visiting her more frequently.

"I did not have an accident," Ronny said, "The man hit me. He was talking to his girlfriend on his cell and smashed into my car."

"At what hour of the night? Tell Sister what a night owl you've become."

"Sister, don't listen to him. William, you are such a gossip. You should be ashamed of yourself. Why would anyone want to go to confession to you--you are such a tattletale?"

"See how he is, Sister?" Laughlin said.

She was smiling, but it was the weakest of smiles. Laughlin felt like someone had just punched him in the stomach.

"I will be back. God bless you, Sister. Pray for us."

"Yes, Sister, pray for him that he watches his big mouth a little more. It is always a delight to see you, Sur Margarita. God bless you. I will be praying for you."

Of course he mispronounces "Sor." 'You're a liar, though, Mr. Dry Cleaner, because it was no delight to see her.' Ron hated seeing sick people. *But it was a good lie, or at least made with good intention. That seemed a contradiction inherent in pastoral life. You faked it, and it helped people.*

His cell went off again. He walked out into the corridor. It was Carl Sand.

"Hey Father, what is this &#%! about the postponement of the wedding? I mean, I'm sorry to swear at you, but I would think you'd at least say something to me if there's been a postponement."

You're not swearing anything, bucko, you are just being vulgar.

"I don't know what you mean, Carl. The sign was supposed to say that the wedding was cancelled."

"That's what I thought," he said. *But not what you hoped.*

"I will check on it. What time is it?"

"It's 11:30, some people just got there early for the wedding. They called me, well, actually, they called one of my groomsmen."

He still has groomsmen?

"I'm on my way to the parish. Right now I'm in the hospital visiting a nun," said Laughlin.

That was a nice touch. I probably should have added, "Who is dying of cancer".

"Ok, then, let me know what the problem was," he said.

Now you're back to your executive mode. You were the one who had hoped in some way that it was only a postponement. Poor bastard.

"One of the idiots at the parish put a sign saying that the wedding was postponed," he explained to Ron, who was looking at him oddly.

"You're going to the parish to see what the sign says?"

"It will take fifteen minutes. Can you wait that much for lunch?"

"Why sure, if it's necessary. I don't understand why you can't just call."

So he called. That was worse than going there.

"Holy Trinity," said a bored voice of a teenager.

"Donna Marie?" he asked.

"Holy Trinity," she said.

"Donna Marie, is that you? This is Father Laughlin," he said.

"People have been looking for you," she said.

"What for?"

"People have been looking for you for the wedding at noon."

"There is no wedding at noon, it's been postponed, I mean cancelled. Didn't they put a sign on the door of the church? Marilu told me she was going to put a sign."

"What sign?"

The girl is an idiot. She is going to give me a stroke one day.

"The sign about it being cancelled, the wedding?"

"It said postponed."

"Why did it say postponed? It was supposed to say cancelled."

"Same thing," said the young girl with all the wisdom of her less than twenty years of being a spoiled brat.

"No, it is not the same thing," he said.

"You just said it was postponed," she said, hurt now that he was insisting.

"I meant to say it was cancelled. Didn't Marilu put the right sign on the door?"

"She was in a hurry and she asked me to do it."

"And which sign did you put on the door?"

Ron was laughing at this point. It amused him to see his friend in a "who's on first" conversation with a ditzy teenager.

"I put the wedding was postponed."

"Why did you put that?"

"Because I couldn't remember what she said. I knew it was one of the two, postponed or cancelled, so I thought postponed sounded better. Not so harsh."

Not so harsh!

He hung up, and then he realized that he would have to go to the church. It was already twenty to twelve. His phone rang. It was Donna Marie.

"Father, these people are looking for you."

"What do they want?"

"They want to know what happened about the wedding."

"That's none of their business."

He now heard her saying to the people, "Father Laughlin says that it's none of your business."

"Donna Marie! What are you saying? I can't believe you would say something like that to people. Tell them there was a problem, and they will be informed in due course."

He heard her repeat the message.

"They want to know when is 'in due course.'"

"Donna Marie, go to the church, rip off the signs and call it a day."

He hung up. She called again.

"Father, do you mean I can go home?"

"You would have to ask Father Jako for that."

"But you said, 'call it a day.'"

"That was because you have already made your share of big mistakes for a week. Stop complicating things."

"Whoa," said Ron. "William, don't hold back!" He was completely amused.

"The girl is like some kind of New Jersey Valley Girl. Telling people what I said to her over the phone. She has no common sense. No wonder Jako thinks the world of her. They must be from the same planet."

"Patience, my child," said Ron, chuckling. "You are cute when you are mad; you have the desperate air about you, like a kid caught in a lie."

"Get in the car; we better do a drive-by on the parish."

Laughlin's heart sank when he saw the group of people on the steps of the church. They were dressed for a wedding. He parked the car on the street and walked over to the sign on the door.

"Sand--Horvath wedding postponed," he read, and said, "Oh no," audibly.

"Father, Father, we have a question for you." An aggressive lady was homing in on him.

"Yes?" *I will act like an idiot. That way I can kind of blend in.*

"We are here for a wedding, and no one else seems to have shown up. Then we see this sign about a postponement. Maybe you can clear up this mystery."

"I am only the priest, ma'am," he said. "You will have to ask them about it, I mean the parties involved."

The woman, about forty-five years old, dressed to the nines, with a good, although ample, figure, was not satisfied with this answer. She frowned, as though she was trying very hard to understand the priest.

"I have come here from Queens; you have no idea what a surprise this is to me."

"I can only imagine," said Laughlin. *She wants the dirt.*

"I thought something was happening at the shower. She had the poor boy there; he obviously didn't know how to act in front of all those women and girls. It was strange. I thought, you know, something here is not right."

So, Miss Marple, you shouldn't be so surprised, Laughlin wanted to say.

"Can you tell me who cancelled? Was it him or her?"

"We had a meeting, both were there."

She sensed that she had hit a wall. Her green eyes focused on him a minute; her brows were tightened in little arches. *How much does she spend on makeup, and how much time to ladle it all on?*

"Oh well, this is one for the books. I've got my invitation anyway, and we took a picture of the sign," she said and shrugged her shoulders. This caused some movement of her shoulders, with effects on the ensemble that the priest did his best to ignore. He thought of John XXIII and the Parisian lady, when the then Cardinal Nuncio had offered an apple to her since she was dressed like Eve.

"God bless you," said Laughlin.

"Let's go," said the woman.

Her hair is dyed. She probably has the Irish curse of going gray or white early.

The others in her party — a woman about her age, possibly a sister — who looked a bit dowdier than the interrogator, two teenaged girls and a balding guy in a suit who was probably the brother-in-law looked at her.

"Father's lips are sealed. We won't get anything out of him," she said, "So let's get going."

Laughlin laughed despite himself. *Ron will enjoy this, he thought.*

After he saw their SUV pull out of the parking lot, he ripped down the sign.

Chapter Five

*I'll take you to a place that is special," he said to Ron, "so that you can stop deriding Zachary and start recognizing it as a cosmopolitan town."

"Cosmopolitan?' asked Ron.

"It is a Salvadoran restaurant. You will like it, it has beef and shrimp and stuff. And really reasonable prices."

"I thought you said it was Cuban."

"I figured you'd understand that better."

"Why?"

"Because of South Beach. Never mind. You'll like this place and it's very economical."

"That part is what attracts you, William, but that's ok. I am like St. Paul; I have lived rich and lived poor."

"The second part of the phrase should be in the future tense."

"Didn't your mother ever teach you manners? I am going to have to call her."

"She'll be glad to talk to you," said Laughlin, "She is on a new kick now. Why did I ever leave Ohio? She sounds like that musical, was it *On the Town* or something? You know Broadway musicals. I could have been a priest in the Youngstown diocese and be close to home."

"What did you tell her?"

"I said that it was your fault. When we studied at Seton Hall, you said you would only continue in the seminary if I stayed in New Jersey."

"You are horrible, William. Why would you say that to your mother? She's going to be mad at me!"

"Well, first of all, it is true. Remember when I went to the interview with Youngstown? You told me before I left that I might not find you when I came back. Even though it was second semester of senior year, you were thinking of leaving."

"You have a terrible memory, Child."

"I remember it exactly. I was packing my suitcase and you came and sat on my bed, practically knocking it over. You were whining. You were wearing those pants with the bell bottoms, remember the ones you had patched because of the chafing? I have a good memory."

"If it's good, why do you only remember the most embarrassing things?"

"So you remember, too."

"I do, but I don't know why you have to dig up all this stuff from the past. My present is hard enough, without looking for past mistakes. Those pants."

"It's ok, I like New Jersey enough. It ought to save me time in Purgatory."

"You're probably right. I should have gone back to Greenville long time ago."

"Back to whom?"

"That's the thing. Well, one sister is still there, Nanny Ruth."

"What do your siblings think about you leaving the priesthood?"

"William, do you think you can talk a little more discreetly? We are in public."

They were sitting at a table in the restaurant *"El Salvadoreño."* Ron had just ordered a shrimp cocktail and some kind of fruit punch that came in a glass that looked like it should have goldfish swimming around in it.

"William, I need to talk to you about something very serious. But you must promise me, scout's honor, that you won't laugh at me or think that I'm crazy."

"More than I do already?"

"William, I'm serious. Scout's honor?"

"I was never a scout. I always had a fear about going to campouts."

"I wasn't either, but I thought all you bourgeois white boys went to the scouts."

"No, and you know I'm not bourgeois."

"Are you listening to me?"

"Yeah, why are you in such a funny mood?"

"I assure you, William, you would be in a different mood if what is happening to me were happening to you."

He is tucking into the cocktail as though he had not eaten in a week.

His phone started vibrating again.

"Hello," said Laughlin.

I lied. I really don't want to greet anyone.

"Well, hello, William, how are you?"

"Jordan? What a surprise!" Ron looked up from the jumbo shrimp on his fork that he was about to put into his mouth. He did not seem to recognize with whom Laughlin was speaking. *What's with the blank stare?*

"Yes, William, I am calling from my nephew's yacht on my niece's phone. We are up near Kennebunkport."

"I knew you would be about some pastoral task."

"Well, actually, I am. Tomorrow I am to marry my nephew's brother-in-law. At least, I will have the Mass. It is possible that his father the deacon will witness the actual exchange of vows. He is from the state of Massachusetts. Anyway, the pastor will be there and has both jurisdiction and certification by the Sovereign State of Maine."

"Sounds like quite a wedding."

"What wedding?" said Ron, in a strange sounding

voice.

"His nephew's brother-in-law's wedding,"

This drew a complete blank from Ron, who then pushed another whole shrimp into his face.

"What's going on?" asked Jordan.

"I am sitting at lunch in a Salvadoran restaurant in downtown Zachary, New Jersey, with our good friend Ronald Avery."

"Wonderful," said the other, and something else that was lost.

"It's Jordan McCabe," Laughlin said to Ron. Name recognition was not apparent.

"What's that?" asked Jordan. *They must be pulling away from the shore,* he thought, *we're losing the signal.*

"I was telling Ron who you were. He is so famished; he seems to be oblivious to everything."

Laughlin looked at Ron a bit sternly, but was alarmed when the other looked scared.

"What have you been reading?"

This was so like Jordan. He always wanted to know what you were reading, even when he was braving the wind and waves in the Atlantic.

"Urs van Balthasar."

"Interesting. You always go for the exotic."

"The aesthetic, we could say. Actually, you would like the thing; it is von Balthasar on Barth."

"Reading heretics. In my day, such things were frowned upon."

"Reading about heretics, Jordan? You always talked to us about them." he said.

"What the hell are you talking about?" asked Ron.

Jordan said something Laughlin could not understand.

"Oh?" Laughlin replied.

"Agatha Christie. Much more reliable."

He must be talking about what he is reading, which I did

not ask.

"She wrote enough." He was shouting now, because the connection was not good. The waiter, who looked like he had not been in the U.S. a long time, was looking at him curiously. Laughlin saw that Ron was laughing and that he and the waiter had exchanged a look. Then the connection went dead.

"He is out on the Atlantic in Maine," he said to Ron. "I wonder what that kind of phone call costs."

"Probably free weekend long distance. Lots of companies have it. He sure keeps up with you, doesn't he? Does he still think he can still make a friar of you?"

Suddenly, Ronald is back to normal.

"No, well, I don't know. He is just really loyal."

"But he's not your best friend."

"He is one of them."

"William, you remember when we read *The Chosen* at Seton Hall?"

"I guess so."

"What was the theme? You can only have one best friend. Remember? And that is me."

"Of course, I knew that, I was going to say that; it was on the tip of my old tongue."

The meat dish arrived, a twelve-ounce steak for Ron, with huge onion rings on the side (naturally, a special order). Laughlin was amazed again at the way Ron was eating.

"Now, William," he said, "I am going to resume our conversation before we were so rudely interrupted."

The phone went off again. It was Donna Marie.

"Yes," Laughlin said testily.

"Father, Carl Sand is here to see you. He says he had an appointment with you."

"No, he doesn't have an appointment with me. But don't tell him that! Why don't you tell him to come back in about an hour and a half?"

He heard Donna Marie tell Sand that he should come back. The voice of the other was muffled and he couldn't understand what was being said.

"Father, he says that he'll wait for you."

"Ok, let him into my office," said Laughlin.

"Father?"

"Yes, Donna Marie?'

"He is kinda upset."

"Uh-huh?"

"Do you think I should let him in your office?"

"Yes, Donna Marie." The iron came back into Laughlin's voice.

"Okey dokey," said Donna Marie, and hung up.

"I can't believe it. She said 'okey dokey'."

"She probably meant that it would be alright," said Ron gravely.

"I know what it means. I just can't believe the girl talks like that. She is almost twenty years old, I think. She is studying 'design' in college. Whatever that is."

"William, I sense that you are changing the subject on me. It is very important that you listen to me now."

The phone rang again.

"Donna Marie?"

"Father?"

"What is it?"

"He threw up."

"What?"

"Carl Sand. He threw up all over the place. We were on our way to your office, and then it just gushed out. I think he had too much to drink or something."

"Oh God, he threw up!" said Laughlin to Ron, who was grimacing at him.

"I know," said Donna Marie.

"I wasn't talking to you," Laughlin said.

"He said he is coming back later."

"Sounds like a good idea."

"What should I do now?"

"What do you mean, Donna?"

"I mean, like it's really smelling bad here."

"And your question is what should you do?"

"Uh-huh. Is like somebody going to come and clean up this stuff?"

"I think the bishop is going to stop by and tidy up a bit."

"What?"

"*You* are going to clean it up, Donna Marie!" The energy with which he said this seemed to frighten Ron. Laughlin forced himself to calm down. "I am sorry, but you are the only one on duty now. Things happen sometimes. There is a mop in the closet. Throw some water and soap on the stuff. Please clean it up. It was an accident."

"It's really yucky and smells like beer," said Donna Marie.

"Life is like that sometimes," he said. "Thanks for helping out."

Ron had stood up and he reached over to take Laughlin's phone.

"No more phone calls until we are through," said Ron in a tone of voice that Laughlin did not recognize.

"I am sorry, Ronny," he said. "Go ahead, tell me. But please sit down."

"William, do you remember Abdul Duke?"

"Who could forget him? I thought he was from Africa because of the name. There were those Africans from Nigeria, remember?"

"He is trying to get me arrested."

"What?"

"You remember we worked together briefly."

"Yeah, at the McDonald's."

"Very good, you remember. Well, he began to be insanely jealous of me. He has now informed the F.B.I. that

I am a cocaine smuggler. As a result, I am being followed."

"Followed?"

"I suppose you have not heard the helicopter just now?"

"The helicopter?"

"It followed me up from Trenton. It's above us now."

"It is probably coming from the airport. Some VIP. This is a joke, right?"

"I'm not joking, William. It's very urgent that you understand what I'm saying. I thought that changing to your car would avoid their attention, but somehow they have been able to detect us here."

"Ronny, you're crazy," Laughlin said.

"William, I wish I were. How could they have followed us here? I got it! Your cell. There must be some kind of chip they are homing in on."

"Ron, you are kidding, right?"

"I wish I were, my brother," he said, and his face looked like that of a man who had just lost his soul.

He is probably in diabetic shock, thought Laughlin suddenly. *Sugar can make you paranoid and incoherent.* His sister the nurse had told him that.

"They have been following me for weeks."

"That can't be, Ronny. They could have arrested you by now."

"They think they're going to catch me with drugs."

"But you aren't dealing drugs."

"No, but they'll plant some on me. You don't know about these things. Nobody does until he gets caught up in them."

He is crazy. His mind is overthrown, like somebody says in King Lear.

"Do you be- be- be- be-lieve me?"

He stutters when he is nervous. This is heart-breaking.

"Of course I do," Laughlin lied.

"Of course I do, of course you do, of course you do," said Ron and stood up.

"Ronny, are you feeling alright? You don't look so well."

"I'm, I'm, I'm—what did you say? There is, you see, this other thing, you know, I think you can see, I am sure that you could if you wanted to do so."

"Ronny, why are you standing up?"

"Aren't we going?"

"I haven't paid the check yet. Just wait a minute."

Nor have we eaten our lunches completely. I have to take him to the hospital.

"Where are you going, William? Don't leave me."

"I am going to pay the check. I'll be right back."

Ron was looking around the place as though he had not noticed where he was until that moment. The owner came up hurriedly to William.

"Is something wrong?" he asked. "Food is no good?"

"Everything is fine. I'm just going to take my friend to see a doctor. He is feeling dizzy."

I wonder if he knows the word dizzy. The poor man was upset we were leaving. I should have said 'vertigo'. That's the same in Spanish.

"No pay this time," he said, "You friend sick."

Ron was behind Laughlin and overheard.

"I'm not sick, I just, I just can't remember. Where are we going now?" *Ronny has a catatonic look.*

"I thought we would swing by the emergency room to have them check out your blood sugar. Have you checked yourself lately?"

"No, not really. I…"

Laughlin thought that he might give him a battle about going to the hospital, but Ron was suddenly very docile. They didn't talk on the short drive. The nurses were very business-like when he tried to describe what was happening to his friend. He felt that they were discounting whatever he said because he was not using the right vocabulary, which happens a lot in life. *You don't say "Open Sesame" and the cave entrance doesn't appear.* However, once they had taken Ron's blood pressure and a test for the sugar, there was a great change in attitude.

They guided them both to the rooms behind the desk, well ahead of other people who were waiting there. Ron laid down immediately when they brought him to the cubicle, which surprised Laughlin. *He must feel awful bad to put up with this whole rodeo.* They had Ron in a gown in a few minutes, and when Laughlin asked an orderly forty minutes later what they would be doing and how long it would last (he thought they would give Ron a shot of insulin and dismiss him) the young man said, "He's a keeper."

"What?" asked Laughlin, who really had not heard the last word.

"He's a keeper; your friend is going to have to stay here."

Fortunately, Ron had already closed his eyes. Laughlin said he would be back a little later and left. His friend had moaned something like "thank you." Leaving the Emergency Room entrance, Laughlin wondered if he should go into the hospital again and greet Sister Margarita, but decided against it. He would not have much to say, would want to leave almost immediately, and the other would be upset.

He got into his car, and said to himself, "This is quite an interesting day."

Bad habit, he thought, *talking to myself out loud.*

Chapter Six

The first thing that he noticed about the office was, of course, the smell. Donna Marie, in an inspired piece of revenge, had apparently cleaned up the vomit from the carpeting and deposited it in the wastebasket under the secretary's desk Whether this was a gesture against the secretary or against Laughlin was hard to assess. She had mopped up the floor, apparently, as there were swirling patterns of a kind of sediment made of soap and human regurgitation. Laughlin methodically took the waste out to the dumpster, rinsed the wastebasket, and returned to the office. Because Donna Marie had the air conditioning turned on, the priest turned it off and opened some windows. An acrid smell still hung in the air.

Donna Marie, you are a prize.

He went into his own office, which was actually bigger than the pastor's. It also had a bathroom, a very narrow one he called his water closet, which was a reminder of the previous pastor's kidney problems, according to Louis Bertrand Jako, Esquire, who didn't want the office because it was "exposed to the outside". "I don't want them knowing my whereabouts," he said, and the pastor's office had an escape route up the stairs. The smell was less strong in this room, but it had invaded there, too. If only he had told Donna Marie to let Carl into the restroom, he would have been saved a great deal of effort. But of course, Donna Marie would not have guided a vomiting man to the restroom, since it was more convenient to sit at the desk in shock.

Back in the outer office, the smell persisted. The priest even looked around for vomit on the floor. *Maybe he had some kind of projectile thing going on.* He went back to his desk, leaving his office door open because the ventilation from several windows might help.

He opened the window that "exposed" his office to the street, in Jako's calculations. It came to him that he would have to preach at the Neo-Cat Mass. The pastor was giving the financial report at the other Masses, but no pitch on niggardliness to the "Spanish." Laughlin sat at his desk and looked at another book of spiritual reading. He had several around the house. *I am certainly not tearing through this.* He looked at a part he had underlined.

"…the sad spectacle of a priest reduced to the condition of a poor wretch who sinks so low as to pick up with great eagerness the crumbs that fall from the world's table, so laden with attractive things for its own intimates." *I remember the words of this song from when I was a young man in the seminary, but I have forgotten its melody.*

Nature called, and he went into his bathroom. Because the door to his office was half closed, and no one was in the outer office, he did not close the door to the bathroom. That is why he was surprised to hear a woman's voice in the office.

"Father, hello Father, are you there?"

It was Priscilla Bidener. *Who let her in?*

"Father?" It was a desperate voice.

"Priscilla, where are you?" he asked. He fixed his pants and came out of the bathroom.

"I am at the window."

Thank God at least I have preserved my modesty. Wait till I tell Ronny this one.

"Father, is that you?" Her voice could not have been designed to grate on his nerves more than it did.

"I wish it wasn't, actually," he said.

"Why are you hiding from me?" she asked in a cheery voice.

Maybe because I was involved in an activity that I generally like to keep private.

"Here I am, Priscilla, how are you?" Laughlin was now standing at the window. She was used to the light outside and did not see well into the office, which was still relatively dark.

"I am fine. Can I come in?"

"I am afraid not, Priscilla. We have had a kind of incident here and someone was sick all over the place. It is not a great atmosphere. Are you here to pray your rosaries for me?"

"Who said they were for you?"

She is perky today.

"Let's see, I think you told me that you pray three rosaries for me each day."

"I might stop saying them."

"Oh no, Priscilla! Don't tell me you are going to pray them for Fr. Jako."

"Him? I am not going to pray for him!"

"Where charity and love prevail, there God is ever found," he sang out to her.

This is absurd. I am singing a hymn to a crazy woman who practically stalks me and is right now at my window, peering in with no shame and only limited by acute myopia.

"What the hell happened here?"

Laughlin heard the voice and started. It was Jako reacting the *odeur* of the outer office.

"I'm in here," he shouted back, a bit too loudly.

"I said did you want me to come in?" said Priscilla at

the window.

"No, don't come in," he said to her.

At the same time Jako was lightly knocking at the door of the office, which was ajar, and entering at the same time. The pastor stopped halfway through the door.

"Why did you say you're here and not want me to come in? Are you with someone?"

"Who is that?" said Priscilla, who was staring through the window screen like a cross between Mr. Magoo and an eagle.

"It's Father Jako," Laughlin said.

"Of course it's me," said Jako, who came into the office. "Who is at the window?"

"It's Priscilla Bidener," said Laughlin, who felt like a child caught stealing cookies from the jar in the kitchen.

Priscilla, overwhelmed by the movement of the pastor toward the window, had ducked down. All that could be seen of her was the seat of her polyester pants.

"Who is this Juliet at the window with Romeo?" asked Jako.

Laughlin noticed that Priscilla was swaying with laughter in her awkward position of being doubled over. *She thinks it's funny and she thinks the pastor cannot see her.*

"What the hell is that? Are you doing the weeding, Priscilla Bidener? Do you think I can't see your rear end among the bushes? Stand up straight."

She reluctantly pulled herself up.

"What is this about? Father Laughlin has enough on his mind with the cancelled wedding and friends visiting him to be talking through the window at you. Now go over to say your prayers or go home."

"I am on my way. All I was doing was saying hello," she said sheepishly.

These two have known each other for years and one is just as bad as the other.

They were alone in the office. Laughlin looked up at his boss.

"What is it with the office? Did the cleaning lady discover ammonia or something?"

What if I acted like I didn't know? Would the old guy figure it out later?

"The would-be groom came to the office about an hour after the wedding that was supposed to be. He had drunk a few beers on his golf outing and he suddenly felt a little sick. I wasn't here because I had to take Ron to the Emergency Room at Trinitas. I told Donna Marie to clean it up but she left the vomit in Carol's wastebasket."

"Carol, you mean our secretary Carol?" Jako started laughing. "You really know how to collect them; I will tell you that, Laughlin."

You will tell me that again, *that is. I might add, however, that Donna Marie was your choice for weekend secretary.*

"I have to go up and catch up on the news," said Jako.

What could be so interesting?

"I have to do something about this vomit smell," Laughlin heard himself say this, and could hardly believe it; he was beginning to talk to himself.

"Well, carry on, Romeo; watch out for that Juliet, however---she used to stalk poor Stashu, too." Stashu was Stanley Bronkowicz, a former associate pastor at Holy Trinity who had left to get married. *Jako really liked that guy; he is always talking about him.*

"I told you about Stashu, didn't I? He was like fly paper to the women. He was a magnet for broken hearts and the hot to trot. Poor sucker. I took all the women's renewals because he had I guess you could call it an Achilles heel."

Jako smiled. *He's not going to expand on the body metaphor this time,* thought Laughlin. *He has told me that joke several times.*

The old priest looked on the verge of saying something,

and then turned.

"Good luck with the Spanish people at the Catechumen Mass," he said over his shoulder.

"No such thing as luck, Father, you know that is one of my fixed ideas."

If I say "idées fixes" like I would more naturally, he would make a face, like when I asked at the diner if they had grey poupon mustard.

"You're like an old friend of mine," said Jako, "He said the only kind of luck he had was bad, so no use wishing."

He is getting soft on me. This last remark was kind of paternal, in a strangely shy way.

"I am going to see if the Chink wants to go out to eat-- I'm going to skip the K of C because they are having Gurnik cater again. That guy can't cook worth a damn. Mashed potatoes and stuffed cabbage, too much tomato sauce, not enough whip in the potatoes." said Jako.

Jako knew his food. We are always going out to eat, thought the priest. Why couldn't we get a cook, like some other parishes?

Jako was at the door and looking at Laughlin over his shoulder.

"By the way, where is your friend Ron?"

"I told you, he's in the hospital. His blood sugar shot up at the meal and I took him to emergency. They said he had to stay."

Jako turned to look at Laughlin.

"Where did you eat?"

"El Salvadoreño," he said. *He is going to react to that with some smartass remark.*

"You live dangerously. Poor Ronny Avery. He's got sugar, too."

Like you, boss, thought Laughlin, *and without going to Thailand.*

"High blood pressure also," he said.

"Same as me, wonders never cease. I got my sugar from

CHAPTER SIX   63

those damn Buddhist shrines. They keep giving you water, wells of life or something like that. I drank a bit at every one of those goddamned places. The little monks probably knew it would get to me."

The ever-popular story of his trip to the Orient with his nephew. Laughlin had never seen the nephew and wondered if he was still in touch with his uncle. It must have been a lot of dough to take somebody to Hong Kong, Singapore, Thailand and Ceylon (Jako didn't like to say Sri Lanka; his mind was set in the geography maps from his days in school). The only thing he ever said about the trip was about the water. Jako never took the priests out to Chinese or Thai food, so what had he eaten on the trip?

The pastor had turned around now, and was standing in the doorway, his back to the other priest.

This is an existential moment. Jako is very paternally paying me special attention, in spite of the vomit smell. He isn't angry and is visibly concerned about my friend, even though possibly, that is because he has the same infirmities. This was something to file away. He was like a kid wanting to make friends, hanging around the door, joking about the little monks in Thailand, giving him holy water to drink. *Why the hell would he drink it? Probably thought it would have magical properties. Superstitious.*

"Father," it was Priscilla again. She had thought Jako was out of earshot. Probably she had been listening at the window again. *Had she crawled to the window commando style? This woman is like some kind of senior citizen version of* Fatal Attraction.

Jako heard her. He turned around and moved surprisingly swiftly to the window.

"Now that is enough, Priscilla Bidener. You can go right to your car. I do not want to see you when I go out the door of the rectory. If necessary, I will escort you to your car. If not, I will call the police. I will get a restraining order.

Do you know what harassment is?"

Priscilla was looking in the window like an animal caught in the headlights of a semi trying to remember the words of the act of contrition.

"I said, 'Do you hear me?'" shouted Jako.

He really hadn't said it, of course, but thought he did. But it has done the job. Priscilla was skulking off to the parking lot.

"I don't want you here until tomorrow at Mass!" shouted Jako again.

"She is just a lost soul," said Laughlin. *I feel like one myself around here.*

"Well, she better get lost, I'm telling you. Humph. It's her husband's fault. Joe Bidener was the evilest man I ever met. Treated her like the proverbial you-know- what. Knocked the sense out of her. If you ever want an example of a battered wife, you've got it there."

Jako cleared his throat as he walked out of the office.

Chapter Seven

I better prepare for Mass with the Neo-Catechumens, he thought. Laughlin's Spanish was decent but not fluid. Normally, he read the scriptures for the Mass aloud several times during the week to practice for the Mass. This week, he had not had the time. Maybe he would let the Neo-Catechumens go on and on about the readings, because he was really not up to saying anything. The Cats, as he called them, liked to do almost rabbinic exegesis of texts, each taking one word and then wrapping their thoughts about themselves around it.

Just as he thought this, the phone rang, this time the parish line. He forgot that Saturdays in the afternoon the phone went straight to a message about the times of the Masses. He picked up the phone too late, said hello, and then heard Mary Horvath's voice saying, "Father?" The tape had already started rolling, however.

Jako's voice slowly read out all the Mass times, and Mary repeated Laughlin's name several times. *Doesn't she know a parish has a tape machine connected to the phone on weekends?*

There was a call on the next line. He assumed it was Mary, who had listened to the number for emergencies.

"Mary?"

"No," said a woman's voice that sounded surprised.

"I'm sorry, whom were you calling?"

"Isn't this Holy Trinity Church?"

"Yes it is, how can I help you?"

"But you answered so strangely. Who is Mary?"

Oh shoot, he thought.

"She's my sister. I thought she was calling me," he said. *Not really a lie,* he argued to himself, because Mary Horvath was a sister in Christ. Also, he had a sister who was named Helen Mary, back in Ohio. That counted for something.

"Oh," said the voice, a little mollified, but still quite steely.

"How can I help you?" *Now, I go on the offensive,* he thought.

"I am at a Motel 8 near the freeway. I guess I missed the Mass this afternoon."

"Which Mass did you miss?"

"The one for Mary Horvath and Carl Sand."

Uh-oh.

"It's been cancelled." He tried to make his voice sound matter of fact.

"Cancelled?"

"Yes, ma'am. They decided not to marry. Sometimes it is better that way."

Where the hell did that come from? Sometimes it is better that way? Better than what. How was it a "way"?

"Oh my God," said the woman.

Quick, counselling skills, he thought, *reflect back!*

"That upsets you."

"No, it's just that we have come here from Nanty Glo, Pennsylvania-- do you know where that is? Way on the other side of the state. Near Johnstown, my husband is saying, that's him talking in the background, he says you probably heard of Johnstown. But the weird thing is my mother. She said today, 'Where are you going?' She is kinda losing it, so I told her; we are going to Mary Horvath's wedding, Joe Horvath's daughter.

"She says, 'But she is not getting married today.' I say, 'Sure she is Ma; I'll show you the invitation.' She looked at it and then said, 'You'll see.'"

"Did someone call her?" Father Laughlin asked innocently.

"No one called her. Who would call her? She just knew it."

Ok, don't get upset. You said the old girl was losing her marbles. Maybe there was a call and she forgot to tell you.

"Why did you say there was a call? My husband wants to know."

This, then, had been the subject of a muttered conversation

"No, I don't know anything. I was just speculating."

She wants the extra sensory explanation, and you start being a Sherlock Holmes about it. Sound the retreat!

"So what are we supposed to do? We have the gift in the trunk of the car."

You aren't going to say, 'Can't you return it?' because that will only prolong this conversation.

His cell started ringing, or rather, humming. It was Mary Horvath.

"Maybe you should try to contact the family later in the week. It was last minute. Um, I have a call coming in on the other line."

"Do you know where I can getta hold of Mary?"

"Not really," he said.

She could be calling from Florida for all I know, so it is not a lie.

"He doesn't want to tell us," Laughlin heard the woman tell her husband.

The man is probably another ace, married to her.

"I really have to go, I have a call on another line," the priest said abruptly. *Why should I be nice to her when she is calling me a liar? Of course, I am kind of lying to her. All these*

years and so many books read, and even more bought, and I am
still saying "kind of."

"Mary," he said into his cell.

"It's not Mary," said George. "I am sorry that I tricked
you."

He sounds awfully calm, but then he was just the author of
the drama today, not one of the principal actors.

"You didn't trick me. Actually, you saved me from a
lie. Some of Mary's family was calling me from a Motel 8
near the freeway."

Laughlin heard this relayed to Mary in George's flat
voice, completely toneless, like one of those understated
comedians that were popular in the eighties.

"Who was it?"

This was now Mary.

"Somebody who lived in some place called Nanty
Glo," said Laughlin.

"Oh my God, it was Maureen. Didn't her mother tell
her? I made a special call just to let her know."

There goes the Twilight Zone interpretation of how the
mother knew, thought Laughlin. He had to stifle a chuckle.

"Father, George and I want to come in and talk," said
Mary.

"Sure," said Laughlin.

They cannot be thinking of today.

"Are you doing anything now?"

"Now?" he asked.

"Well, yeah, like now."

"I was just getting down to preparing my homily in
Spanish."

No noise on the other side.

"Then I have confessions," he said, suddenly recalling
the same.

"How about later?" asked Mary, with what seemed
exaggerated patience.

"I have the Spanish Mass from 8:00 to maybe 9:30 tonight."

"We'll be here at confessions, then. They're done at 4:30, right? George really needs to talk about this whole thing. I have been too much of a witch all day."

And rightly so, cancelling a wedding.

"Sure, I mean, not about the witch part. But maybe we could meet tomorrow."

"Oh Father, we really need to talk to you. Just five minutes."

"I have an hour of confessions then another Mass at 8:00 pm. There is a dinner from the Knights of Columbus."

Not that I intend to eat Gurnik's stuffed cabbage.

"We will be your last people for confession. Father, we need you. This is not an everyday kind of thing."

Understatement of the year.

"Mary, I am very sorry for how difficult this day is for all of you, Carl and George, you and your family. Another group was from Queens."

"Oh my God, Aunt Patty."

"I don't know."

"Ok, we'll see you at 4:30 then, good-bye."

He had started to answer when he realized she had hung up.

The priest started to think, budgeting his time. He would give them short shrift, keeping his cool, but emphasizing that the crisis would pass and that they should get some sleep and stop talking about it. Then he remembered the other circumstances complicating his life.

What about Ron? What if they are going to release him? Maybe after Mass, but that was risky.

Sometimes he got the impression that the Neo-Cats wanted to make a night of it. On second thought, tonight it might be better with them.

Chapter Eight

He picked up his *Imitacion de Cristo*, which inspired most of his homilies in Spanish. "¿Toda la vida de Cristo fue cruz y martirio, y tú quieres descansar y gozar?" *Christ's whole life was the cross and martyrdom, and you want to rest and enjoy? Why is that every time I read this little book, it seems to mock me? I wonder how Ron is doing. Can you imagine thinking that a helicopter followed you up from Trenton? Who can I tell that one, too? Maybe his mother, and Ron, that is, when Ron was not talking crazy stuff.*

"Que esperamos de la vida?" he said aloud in the quiet of his office. "Si queremos una vida como Cristo, queremos la cruz."

That is not bad. If we want a life like Christ's, we want the cross. The Hispanics loved talking like that. They did not always live enamoured of sacrifice, but they related to the concept so much better than the Anglos.

He was hungry, something that often happened to him when he was nervous. *Were there cookies in the kitchen? Or maybe he should attack the M&Ms in the TV room? This was really a stressful day, you have to take measures to de-stress yourself,* he thought.

Father Aquino was in the TV room watching EWTN. He was dressed in his collar, which meant that he was going to work as a priest. When he was not "on duty," he wore regular button-down shirts.

"How did it go?"

"What do you mean?" asked Laughlin.

"Your lunch with Father Ron," said Peter, frowning.

He thinks I am an idiot. Which is close to the truth, I am afraid. Of course he would ask about Ron. And call him "Father" Ron.

"Not very good, Ron got sick."

"I thought I smelled something in office," said Peter.

"No, that was not Ron, it was my groom, the guy whose wedding was cancelled."

"The groom showed up?" asked Peter, twisting his eyebrows and the squinting.

"No, well, yes. I mean, he came to the office to see me. He went golfing in the morning with his buddies. They had planned it when there was still going to be a wedding. Evidently, a case of beers was also part of the plan. By the time he got around to visiting me, the guy was probably drunk, and then sick."

"Very bad," said Father Peter.

That is one of his catch phrases. Of course, it was completely appropriate in the circumstances.

"Ron was sick, but it was his diabetes. He got incoherent on me at the Salvadoran restaurant, you remember, the one we went to when Father Jako was on retreat."

"Yes, very good, very much food. Not today?" the other priest asked.

"No, it was not the food. He doesn't inject himself. Insulin, he needs it. The whole thing's a mess. I think his business must be folding too."

"Business folding, too?"

Everything has gone to mierda for old Ron. That was like something he had read in a book, which was it? *Something about "hard cheese on Tony".* Father Peter was quick to react to the business folding. All his Filipino professional friends are prosperous.

"What are you watching?" asked Laughlin.

"Pope in Ukraine," said Father Peter.

It's what you would expect, I suppose. Casts of thousands, or hundreds of thousands, Pope John Paul II on some kind of pilgrimage. That day he was visiting a place where Stalin's minions had murdered 100,000 persons. The secret police. I used to read up on all that stuff. I had a crush on Solzhenitsyn for a while. I never got through the second volume of The Gulag. That book was probably still at his mother's. He knew that he ought to read the Russian writer but somehow found himself re-reading Roth.

"Who would ever have thought the pope would visit a place like that?" he said to Father Peter.

"Not Stalin. He was enemy of the pope."

"The people seem so happy and moved to be with him," Laughlin said.

"That is how it is. You know I was with Pope Paul VI in Manila?"

"Really?"

"I was there when a man knifed him. A crazy man tried to kill pope."

There was something about an assassination attempt. An airport, no?

"You were there, Peter?" he asked the priest.

"I was secretary then of cardinal archbishop. We went to airport for pope. I was here to kitchen from man who knifed the Pope Paul VI."

Amazing that has not come up before. If that had happened to me, I think I would let everyone know I had been there.

He looked at Peter and smiled.

"You were present at such a historical moment. Why didn't you ever say anything about that? Does Father Jako know?"

"That was beginning of problem with Marcos. President Marcos was there. Later he said he gave the man karate chop and made him drop the knife, it was a beautiful Malay dagger."

"What really happened?"

"President Marcos wasn't even close to pope. No karate chop. One of Swiss guards, he pushed the man back, a bishop there held the man, like this."

He is reliving it. You can see it in his eyes. The mime of the bishop holding the assassin means something to him. But he is so modest that he is checking himself, doesn't want to act as if he had any special participation, even though he was calling a president a liar about an assassination attempt on a pope! The world is a global parish.

Peter finished, then got up, still looking toward the television set and watching the pope's slow progress in the crowd of blond Ukrainians, who seemed to be adoring him.

"Time for confessions," Peter said.

Confessions! I forgot about confessions again.

"I'll be right over," he said. "I am going to call the hospital."

"Ok," said Father Peter. *One of his favorite expressions. "Everything ok, yes?"*

As Laughlin ascended the stairs he heard the elevator moving. *Jako,* he thought. *His legs must really bother him because he never takes the stairs any more. What was the guy's real health status?*

At the top of the stairs, because he was trying to move fast, Laughlin missed a step and fell down. *Thank God no one is here. All I need to do today is fall down the stairs and break a leg. Maybe they could put me in the same room with Ronny at the hospital; we could fight like the* Odd Couple. *"Your friend" the little guy in the ER had said. This carpeting is so old and loose, that is why I slipped. The whole place has this seedy quality to it, it needs a makeover but Jako will leave that to his successor. He says that all the time, "I'll leave that to my successor."*

It took some time, but the operator found Ronny's room

number. *No answer, which I should have expected. Most of the time, that is the story of my life, "no answer." I will have to call him between confessions and the Mass. Or maybe I could run over to the hospital after confessions real quick-like. Ten minutes to get there, five minutes on the stairs, if I don't fall, and two minutes with Ronny, five back to parking garage, unless I dare park on the street, ten minutes back to the parish to give communion at the Mass.* A Jako special executive order, all three priests have to give communion at each weekend Mass.

He looked around for a book for the confessional. *Some Saturdays no one comes to confession. "No sinners here, you might say." That was Jako's line from the pulpit, "I say, 'No repentant sinners, which is a tragedy.'"*

What could I read during confessions? I should try the book in the office. I'll have to run by there on my way over and pick it up. Really I should read more of the Imitacion, *but I need something a little easier on my nerves.*

Chapter Nine

As he passed near the vestibule, the doorbell rang. That was unusual on a Saturday afternoon. *Unusual and irritating. More wedding guests?*

A young lady was standing by the doorway. She had light blond hair, cut around her face in a strange style. Her light skin could not hide that she had been crying; there was redness about the eyes, which were a light blue that seemed almost surreal to the priest. A pretty girl, if she were not so obviously troubled. She looked like the Ukrainians crowding around the pope that he had just seen on television.

"Can I help you?" he asked.

The girl made him think of what Jako used to say about the priest with the Achilles' heel. Stashu would have had a difficult time maintaining his professionalism in the face of beautiful feminine desperation.

"Good old Stashu. If it was a good-looking girl at the door, or even an older one, he would turn the charm on." Jako had a way of putting things that could make you laugh. "She could be asking for directions to the nearest gas station and he would have her sit in his office for an hour."

"Are you a priest?" the young woman asked.

What was your first clue, bright eyes, the black clothes, the Roman collar or the fact that when you rang the rectory doorbell

I showed up?

"Yes I am; can I help you?"

"I need to talk to a priest," she said, in a voice that was strangely flat, as if she were repeating something memorized.

This is going to complicate my getting over to the confessions. Jako will be angry again. This is a trick the "Spanish people" as he calls them play. They show up, but not at the right place, even if at the right time. So much of church stuff is right place, right time, everything in order.

Of course, this girl does not look "Spanish," she looks like someone who got lost in Zachary, New Jersey, like she was from Rumson or some cool place with money.

"Why don't you come to my office?" asked Laughlin.

The girl nodded her head, but oddly, as if she were too upset to talk.

This is about some boyfriend.

"What's going on with you?" he asked. She blinked hard, as if surprised by the question. "I mean: why did you want to talk to a priest?"

"I want to go to confession. It has been a long time. It smells nice in here."

Jako must have brought the Glade from his room. He was always spraying Glade around. Ronny said he thought Jako used it instead of deodorant.

"Ok, I'll say it. I had an abortion. I know, I am saying it like, you know, so what? But it is not a thing 'so what' for me. You see there was this guy."

There was always some guy. Why do these girls get involved with these-- guys? The lambs that fell in love with wolves." They don't notice the teeth because of the smile"-- that was another Jako-ism, a take-off on "forest for the trees."

"He was, he is, I guess, well, I don't know. His mother died and his father was my father's boss. He tried to commit suicide, I found out later, thanks for not telling me, everybody! Anyway, his father was a wreck with the death of the mother, and my boyfriend—I mean my ex---was a wreck, too. They lived just the two of them in this mansion ---I mean a real mansion--- because an older sister married somebody out in California and had left years before. The distance really didn't matter, she is supposedly trapped wherever she is and they, this guy, I mean, and her never really got along. I think she probably was escaping from her father."

There is something to be said for creative syntax, he thought. *The worst thing in the double helix approach to talking about it was that it made something simple complex.*

"He was taking tennis lessons at the Club. My parents decided that I would be a good influence for him. His father was incredible, sleeping with all these women, one of them he brought home, and Cyrus found them together. I mean, seeing your Dad naked with some lady he brought home from work? And she was like, this secretary or something. She screamed when she saw the son. He might have been staring at them for a while for all I know, he was, is, so odd sometimes. Cyrus got in the car and came over to the house. That was the start of our... I guess you could call it our relationship."

"I guess you could call it our relationship." That was actually very good. Lots of people could use that line.

She fell silent as suddenly as she had poured out the previous words. "How recent was all this?" Laughlin asked. *This poor kid. The boss's son is bad, get the girl to take him out of his depression—and get into her own.*

"It was last summer, I think, yeah, last year in August. Entering my senior year. My last summer vacation before... whatever. Anyway, he didn't even like me at first. He was cute, I thought, but so into himself. Until that day that he came over, he really had never talked to me. He told me about his mother dying. I knew something about it. My mother had told me Cy's mother was not very 'social.' That was a word for my mother that meant a lot. It actually meant that she was anti-social. Or maybe just that she didn't like my mother. I just thought of that. Maybe because my mother is so, and, like, the lady saw it."

There was another silence. *Tears are forming in her eyes, the forehead gets tight, the teeth clenched; she is struggling with the narrative.*

"My mother didn't even like her. She was very beautiful, which meant Mums would be jealous. And she was supposedly smart. She had published this book of poems when she was young, like in college. Cyrus found it and he used to carry it around. He had the poems like memorized from reading them so much. He said it was his Book of Common Prayer. That's a book they use in church. They're not Catholic."

"They're Episcopalian?" he asked.

"I don't know, maybe, or maybe Anglican, I think. It was a pretty church, almost Catholic. Like all stone and stuff. Like way hidden in the corner was this little chapel, there was even a picture of Mary or something, it was kind of modern. The minister was dressed up but not quite like you guys."

"Dressed up but not quite like you guys." There you see the catechetical preparation of our people. At least they can notice we wear different kind of dresses. I am officially a half hour late for the confessions that started at 3:00 p.m.

"Anyway, his father doesn't believe in anything. He told Cyrus that now that his, well not his mother, but Cyrus's mother died, he wasn't going to think about death again. Which was odd, because he was worried about Cyrus, supposedly. You see, Cyrus tried to kill himself after his mother died. I already told you that, didn't I? It was all hushed up, of course. But my father knew, and of course, my mother, because she dominates my father so much."

This is stream of consciousness or something. I don't know how to guide this at all. She's another East Coast Valley Girl or something, like Donna Marie. She makes one appreciate Donna Marie a bit more.

"So you started 'relating' when he came over."

"Well, it was a big deal. His father had been worried about, well, obviously, that the kid was going to off himself or something. Probably the woman was bothered too, I guess. Like I wonder how long Cyrus was watching them, but, whatever. He would watch porn for, like, hours. So the father was calling all around. For some strange reason, he was so desperate, he called my father. 'My son has disappeared,' he said. He has this really dramatic way of talking. Sometimes Cyrus sounds like him. My father says, 'He's in the TV room with Mandy' or something like that. The man raced over to our house, I mean, he got there just as my father was explaining to us that Cyrus's father had called, the whole nine yards."

The whole nine yards? This girl talks like a movie. A bad movie.

"But you became, er, friends from that time?"

"Sure, he had already told me so much about himself and his relationship with his father. I cried when I was listening to him. He looked so lost. I just wanted to pull him back from wherever he was. His eyes are, like, you would have to see him I guess."

"But you got involved with him."

"So we started seeing each other at the club, not just for tennis, which he never taught me right, anyway. He was good at it, but that doesn't mean he can explain it, so, like, I'm definitely not better at it for the lessons. Anyway things started rolling. My mother had some days when she had other stuff to do, she's a lady that lunches, like that song, and so he started to pick me up and drop me off. We skipped the lessons some days. Then I got pregnant.

Naturally I would be a puker. I had morning sickness to where I couldn't hide it. Then my mother saw a message from Cyrus on my Blackberry.

"She didn't even talk to me first. First thing, like always, her fingers did the walking, the Yellow Pages, looking for abortion doctors like she would interior decorators or something. Of course, this time she didn't consult her friends. She made the appointment without telling me. The same day I heard that Cyrus was going to the military academy, she tells me, 'Tomorrow, I have an appointment for you.' I'm like, 'Appointment for what?' and she's like, 'For our problem.' And I say, 'What problem is that, may I ask?' and she's like, 'Your pregnancy, we want to take care of that right away.'

"She got my father into it. The next morning, he brought me out to the car. She was sitting there fixing her makeup when he came out of the house. Of course she couldn't go to the abortion clinic looking like an old hag. She had to fix herself up."

She hates her mother. Ya think?

"I told my father I wasn't going, he said, 'No arguments honey, it will be over soon. You can't go back to Catholic high school like you are.'"

Catholic high school! This was a nightmare.

"So off to Brooklyn to get rid of it. That same night my godmother arrived from Detroit. They, like, did the abortion in the nick of time, because her being here would have complicated everything. They explained that I didn't go to the airport because I was a little under the weather, killing your baby can get you down. She probably thought I got my period or something."

Here she began to cry. First, her face constricted, then tears started running out of the corner of her eyes and down her cheeks. Then she doubled up in the chair and started a noise like a moaning.

"I'm so sorry, what a nightmare," said Laughlin.

"It was a nightmare, but my godmother was there and so I didn't scream at them and tell them I wished them dead like my baby, but I thought it. Then we had to go out to eat with her, the next day, up at the World Trade Center, because she is from Detroit and the big buildings are, like, impressive to her. I had wanted to go before I knew Cyrus, so this was supposed to be like a treat for me. Dinner on top of the town, for being obedient to them. It was the worse time of my life. I was thinking, 'Like this is so bogus. Towers of bogusness, the view of bogusness, is what I thought. Without Cyrus, of course, he was already in some kind of college prep prison in Pennsylvania. I am sorry, Father."

"Have you ever talked about this to anyone else?" he asked her. *This could be the first time she is getting all this poison out.*

"Like, who would understand? I started to talk about it with some nun at school, and she was, like, one of those liberal ones. She thought I wanted to talk about a woman's right to choose, so she was saying stupid stuff, like 'sometimes the Church doesn't understand for centuries.' I wanted to say that I lived through something like those Chinese women did when they had to abort. The chaplain at the school had this petition about them, the one-child thing, we all signed it, but I felt like such a scum and a hypocrite."

"Did Cyrus know about this?"

"I called him the night I found out about our 'appointment' from my mother. It was his friend's phone-- some kind of secret phone the guys had hidden over there. It took the one who answered it a long time to find Cyrus. So I tell him what was going on. The phone just went dead. He said nothing. Nothing at all. I couldn't believe it. Here was something that was about us and he had nothing to say. Then the phone was blocked for me."

"This is just awful. You have been through a terrible

experience."

She was still doubled up, her blonde hair hanging straight down. At the last part of his words to her, she had begun whining with an awful sad noise that sounded like someone was choking her.

"Eventually, I got something from him. He sent me his mother's book. I suppose that I should be happy that he sent me the poems. It was the original copy, but there was no note. The military academy is in some kind of forest; I don't even know if regular people can go there. Supposedly worse than a prison. His father whisked him away as soon as my father told him what had happened. Cyrus never contacted me through the whole thing. When I first told him that I was pregnant, before my parents knew, he said something dumb, like, 'I didn't want this to happen. After my mother.' Like what is that? What did his mother have to do with what they were doing to me? A note with the book, I mean a piece of paper ripped out of a notebook just said, 'these are my mother's poems,' nothing else."

"You never heard from him again?"

"No, there were no vacations for Thanksgiving or anything from that school. I know because I went to his house. It was like something from a movie, I was so scared. A housekeeper came out of the house. She looked real upset, like nervous. When she went inside I waited a long time. Then Cyrus's father came out, smiling, like 'Oh what a nice surprise this is,' although I could tell he was scared, too. He told me that Cyrus was doing well. Didn't he write me?"

Again, it was too much for her. She began crying.

"Like how could he &#* write to me from the concentration camp the guy sent him to? I wasn't going to tell him about the book. Really, I was shocked how good I took it. I didn't cry, I just said, 'I got some e-mails; he is such a *great* writer.' I was being ironic.' He knew I was lying, but he could not say anything, because he was lying too. Cyrus couldn't write to me; they didn't allow him to; why did his father ask?"

"You have really been ... I guess betrayed is the word." *I wonder what they would say about that in counselling class. You aren't supposed to give opinions.*

She nodded but didn't say anything.

"You really needed to talk about this. I am going to give you absolution. It might take you a while before you feel that this is all behind you. But it is. This was the remedy you needed. Confession. You have to start healing."

"I hate my parents," she said and then looked up at him. *Did she expect me to be startled? I can understand.*

"Naturally, you feel betrayed by them," he started.

"They are such &#%! hypocrites. Yesterday, we had some Jesuit priest over. He is something at a university, not a big-name one. They had him over to talk to me about careers. He is the brother-in-law to some cousin of my mother. She met him at one of her luncheons, and she was 'charmed', as she says. The cousin came too, and the priest was, like, so impressed with us. Like we were this all-American family or something. The whole thing was fake from the gazpacho soup my mother ordered from the gourmet restaurant to this dessert with raspberries that I don't even like."

The phone was ringing. It was the intercom from the sacristy. Marilu was calling him.

"Father, I am so sorry to interrupt you. I know you must be doing something urgent. It is just that Father Jako called me and he wanted you to know that there are some Spanish people here for confessions."

"I have got someone with me right now," Laughlin said.

"I thought so, Father. It is just that Father Jako was so insistent; I really shouldn't have bothered you."

"No, it's ok. I'll be over in a little bit," he said. *She did not seem to react negatively to what I said about going over. We're almost finished. I just have to give her absolution.*

"Listen, I'm sorry, there is always something else going

on here," said Laughlin.

"That's alright, Father, I've got to go, too," she said without resentment. *She is feeling compassion for me because someone is yelling at me.*

They prayed an Our Father, he gave her the absolution and she thanked him. Then she dialed her cell and was talking with someone.

"I am done," she said. "Right now. I will be out. Where are you?"

Laughlin walked the young woman to the door. As soon as they were in the sunshine, a young man got out of a sporty looking car.

Oh no, he thought. *Supposedly, Cyrus was out of the picture, so who was she calling? She probably is involved with some other guy. She did not confess having relations, but it is obvious from the way the young man looks at her that there is more than a platonic thing going on. He is putting up with a visit to a church because this is his girlfriend, the one he sleeps with. Maybe I'm wrong, but I don't believe so.*

The young man was dressed in a knit shirt that clung to the muscles of his chest. *He works out. Do you think the pants could be a little tighter, maybe? The hair cut looks military. Could it be Cyrus? Could she have left that part out?*

"Hey babe," said the boy to the girl. They embraced and kissed passionately. "Better now?" the boy asked.

"Yeah, he's really sweet." She turned toward Laughlin to introduce him to the other man. "Father, this is…" She blushed and Laughlin took it wrong.

"You're Cy-," Laughlin started to say, but the girl saw it coming.

"Father, this is Doug," she said. *Did the guy see I was going to call him Cyrus?*

"Pleased to meet you," said Laughlin.

The young man had a weight-lifter's grip, the skin of his hand so tight it was almost too hard to be flesh. After the handshake, Doug put his arm around her shoulder, and it looked like a gesture of ownership more than protection.

How can she be healed when she is plunging into something that could start it all up again? She seemed so repentant in her own blonde way. She must have a moral blind spot. What's his name, Lonergan, the Jesuit philosopher I used to read. "Scotosis" he called it. A moral blind spot, like some cataract on the moral eyeball that doesn't perceive shape or light or color, can't make anything out. You can have the vision around the thing, but not directly.

"I gotta go, Father. I really appreciate talking to you," she said, "I, like, feel so much better."

All sincerity. Maybe I am wrong about the boyfriend.

"Nice meeting you, sir," said the young man.

Sir? He wasn't even Catholic! But why would Douglas have to be Catholic? God knows where she met him.

"He's not a 'sir,' he's a Father. I mean, really," Mandy was rolling her eyes, smiling at Laughlin as if to emphasize how much more in the know she was.

"Sorry, I didn't know," said Douglas, looking abashed.

They got into the car. *Was it a Ferrari?* Laughlin never knew cars; it was a great challenge to his masculine credibility. Ron was always talking about Lexuses and Mercedes Benzes. It was like Daltonism for Laughlin; he didn't seem to see what others saw easily. *Something I don't catch, it doesn't register for me. I am thinking Ferrari because of that stupid book about the Buddhist monk, who was not. Mindless bestsellers, the intellectual toys of the middle class. Funny how little stupid things stick in your mind, bits of &#%! on the flypaper of memory—was that Bukowski?*

He waved as they left. *Into the valley of death, what was that from Tennyson?* The Charge of the Light Brigade. *The charge of the 'lights" too "lights" for life.*

Chapter Ten

When he entered the church, he saw that some of the "Spanish" as Jako called them, were waiting near his confessional. Just as that registered, he heard a hissing sound. As he turned around, he saw Marilu in the doorway of the sacristy, gesturing for him to enter.

"What's up?" he asked her.

"Just to let you know, the pastor came late and the Spanish people were waiting outside your confessional. He tried to say something to them, I think that they could confess with him, but they didn't understand. You know how grumpy he gets. He went into the confessional, then he came out about fifteen minutes later, and asked if you were here."

"Actually, I was confessing in my office. There was a walk-in."

"Oh Father, I know you're always working. I just wanted you to know. But he likes you, I hope you realize that. We all do. Sometimes I think about how much I would like to talk to you, also, but you are too busy."

"First of all, who is 'he'? Whom are we talking about?"

"Father Jako, of course. He really seems to like you. You get away with much more than anybody. I don't mean it that way. It's just that he lets you do so many things he wouldn't let another do, with the gym and the hall with the Spanish people. And I can tell that way he looks at you that he admires you."

The gym! The boxing match the Mexicans had organized that had caused so much tension. What a mess that had been! I like the indirect way she mentions it. She likes me and she likes Jako. So the two of us have to get along. Her loyalty to Jako is admirable, considering how he treats her. How he treats anyone, I suppose. No, she was like a mother to Jako. She tried to soften the guy's rough edges. With the other women there was always a group that was on the side of the "parochial vicars" against the boss. Marilu was on everybody's side. A parish is like Peyton Place — *that's what mother always says. Too many busy people, his sister said. By "busy" she meant "buttinski." There was always a kind of drama in the intersection of lives. Drama or soap opera? Both.*

"Thanks, and what did you want to talk about?"

"Lots of things. My son, my husband, that lady in Texas who killed her children."

The way she says children betrays that she is from the South. Or maybe not exactly the South. Was it West Virginia or maybe just the western woods of Pennsylvania? The lady who killed her children in Texas! The human misery that CNN always likes to rub in our faces. "Our top story this hour is 'homo lupus homini,' man is a wolf to his fellow man."

"We will have to hash all that over coffee and cookies in the office when the pastor has his day off. I better go confess," he said.

"Oh Father, don't worry about it. You're thinking, 'another needy person'. It's not that bad. I can listen to your homilies and that is enough. One last thing I wanted to tell you. Your groom came by."

"I know; he threw up in the office."

"No, after that. He was in his car just a little bit ago, waiting for you, I guess. He has a nice white car. It might be a Lexus."

Oh great, the groom — who--was--not is now the neighborhood stalker.

"Ok, I better go."

There was a young guy, relatively light-skinned, actually kind of tall, waiting in line. Then Herlinda, who always had a bunch of complaints about her in-laws, with two of her little boys, and another woman, who looked godforsaken, too.

Herlinda greeted him.

"Este muchacho primero, tiene que ir a trabajar."

She is now organizing the confessional line. Just another chore she has taken upon herself.

Inside the confessional, the young man knelt behind the screen, although there was a chair for face to face.

"Padre," he started, and then sobbed.

There you go. This is certainly a good day to sob. I would like to do some sobbing myself, but will have to wait. "I'll sob tomorrow" No, it was 'I'll Cry Tomorrow,' some English actress postponing mourning for her son killed in the war because she heard when she was ready to go on to entertain the troops.

"Take it easy. Whatever you have to say, that is what the confession is for. Just calm down. God knows everything."

"Padre, soy gay."

Does Herlinda know that, or was she just worried about you getting back to work at the Subway or McDonald's or wherever. Immigrants had the lousy jobs, but you had to keep them no matter what. Losing them meant hunger sometimes. He is probably Dominican by the sound of him—no, he's too light. But there are light-skinned ones, too.

"God knows why you have this cross to bear. Don't worry. What happened to you? Were you involved with someone and then broke up? Did your family find out? Or are you frustrated?"

"Can I sit and talk to you?" he asked the priest in Spanish.

Sure, just don't try to make any moves. Who had said that? I think it was Jansen. There was a macho priest for you, tough as nails. He always wanted prison ministry, and that is what he got. The misery suited him, someone said. But Jansen was always joking about homosexual stuff. Somebody had a crush on another. Why am I thinking about that jerk when this guy is still sobbing?

"Please, come and sit," the priest said.

There was a pause, and then the man came from around the division. *He is probably about twenty. Not markedly effeminate, but maybe someone pulled him out of the closet. They would be calling his family down in the DR.* That had happened to one that Laughlin knew. A guy got drunk, started messing around, and then some "friend" calls the guy's aunt and tells him he came out. Some village in the mountains on Hispaniola-Macondo buzzes with the news. A young man hides something since adolescence, and then spills the beans in a moment of stupidity.

"It is ok to cry," Laughlin said, using "ok" even in Spanish.

"Huh?" The young man hadn't been paying attention, and was wondering what Laughlin had said.

"Está bien llorar. A veces no hay otra cosa que hacer."

Actually, that is somewhat poetic. "It's ok to cry. Sometimes there is nothing else you can do."

"Pero no sirve. Ya he llorado."

There's a trump card. It doesn't work; I have already tried it.

Laughlin's phone hummed again. It was an unidentified caller. There was something familiar about the numbers, but he decided not to answer. He listened to the man's story, although he had missed some of it trying to think who was calling him. Initially, after the passage to Florida, the young man had stayed with a cousin of his stepfather. Then he met some friends at work.

"And then they said that we were moving to a new place. Did I want to join them? It was going to an apartment for four people instead of one with eight. I would sleep on the couch in the living room. But it was still better. Plus, I liked Estanislao. He was decent to me."

*And he had not had much of decency by way of other people.
His stepfather, who beat him and his mother, who loved him but...
His biological father, who had wanted him to spy on his mother
and her new mate, and then afterwards had hit him up for money.
But who were the four? Estanislao, his wife, this guy and?*

"Her brother was ok, too. But then he got sick. I took
care of him because my hours were at night and we were
alone together in the daytime. Then some of his friends
started coming over. At first I liked them, they laughed a lot.
But they drank, and then they smoked marijuana. When I
told Estanislao, he kicked his brother-in-law out and so his
wife—well she was not really his wife, just his *compañera*--
was unhappy. I tried to be friends with her, but then she
left. I was alone with Estanislao, and there was more peace,
which made me feel good. I washed his clothes, I cooked
and I cleaned. I guess I was hoping..."

*Yeah, you might as well pause. "Dot dot dot," as Jako would
say, "So it grows in the Garden State." You should probably
never hope.*

"Then he started bringing girls home. Once I was in
his room when he did. I had not gone to work, because I
wanted to see him. Then I hear him on the stairs, and the
voice of a woman, so I went into the bedroom. Then they
are coming into the bedroom. I went into the closet. I stayed
in there while they, you know they..."

Oh no!

"Suficiente," Laughlin said. *But, did they catch him?*

"I was afraid she was going to stay there the night. I
had to go to the bathroom. I was thinking maybe they go
to sleep, but I wasn't sure. But somebody's phone goes
off. Then they leave suddenly, but before, I realize that
I recognize the girl's voice. She is married, I know her
family. I know her husband. I almost screamed. Worse, I
know Estanislao didn't love her."

Good thing you didn't scream. Plus, people might wonder about you being shocked, given the whole voyeur thing in the closet. Naturally it had to be a closet. Life is so clichéd about symbols sometimes. Although, of course, it was shocking.

"What has happened since then?" the priest asked.

"Nothing. There are more girls. I am looking for another place. Estanislao's *compañera* came by one time. They were talking very low when I went into the kitchen. I think if I go, they get back together, her brother comes back. He is very sick. I think it is *SIDA*."

AIDS!

"Do you have any family to take you in right now?"

"My stepfather's cousin says he will take me back. He wants to charge me three times what I used to pay. My sister is in Bronx. I can go there, but there are many people in the house."

Better go with the sister.

"Maybe it is better for you not to be alone. Do you think Estanislao knows how you feel about him? That's very difficult.'

He looked up at the priest suddenly and seemed relieved.

Is he happy that I recognize what he was going through? He thought it would be impossible for me to understand. Ein bisschen verstandis--*Joel Grey in Cabaret. That at least is something, when someone understands. It gets you out of solitary confinement, even if you stay in the same prison.*

"Yo creo que sepa," he said. *I think he might know. That makes Estanislao a manipulator, or did he think that a pat on the back would keep the kid washing his clothes and cooking his meals? Of course now he has the woman back for that. What would Father Jako say about this case? How would Jako react to this confession?* "Queer little guy," *he would say,* "He better get the hell out of there."

"Tienes que salir de allí." *You have to get out of there before you waste more time. You need to reinvent your way of life. Can't you let this stuff go? I don't understand hopeless attractions like this. The Latinos called them "enamoramientos" and consider them as natural as rainy days. Anglos called them crushes, but it was an adolescent thing, and didn't seem to express the pain that Latins feel. In adults, it could get to be something out of Jerry Springer. That murder when the guy on the show came out for his co-worker. Of course the guy had been in the closet listening. Metaphor becomes reality becomes metaphor.*

"Pero cómo lo hago, padre?" He was asking how to leave.

"Go to your sister. Tell her that Estanislao is charging you too much." *The cost is psychological, of course.* "Tell her that you will help out, that you just want to work. Things will change. You need a change." *Fresh air, a girlfriend, or a girl-friend, maybe, a new life. "Wash that man right out of your hair" that is what Ronny would say. He is always telling stories like this. "Friends" who were in crisis, but I never met them.*

"Not much of what you have said is sin. But the bad thoughts, and the negative feelings are not what God wants," he said in Spanish.

Of course the spying in the closet thing was probably not such a good idea, but there were mitigating circumstances.

"I wanted to do harm to myself," said the boy.

Suicide. It comes up so much when there were emotional problems. The problem was how to react. You never wanted to discount something that serious. Sometimes you want to get out the straightjacket or call the police. Now, it depended. A veces, it was serious, a veces, not.

"I tried to cut myself on the wrist. But it didn't work. We didn't have good knives."

A built-in protection of a poor man's kitchen.

"That is a worse sin than your bad thoughts," said Laughlin, "But God forgives you, Jesus said to the woman caught in adultery, 'Go and sin no more'." Laughlin said.

He heard the boy gasp with shock. *The "poor sons of bitches," isn't that what Faulkner said?*

The priest gave the penitent absolution, placing his hand on the young man's head when he said the prayer. The man was sniffling. Laughlin put his hand on the man's shoulder, and felt him tremble. Then the man leaned into him. *Crying on my shoulder. The poor guy. What is going to happen to these people later on?*

"Gracias, Padre, gracias," he said.

The young man got up awkwardly. It looked like he was going to say something else, but stopped himself. The door had not even closed when he heard the voice of Herlinda.

"Tenemos que ir porque venimos juntos," she said. *We have to go because we came together. Carpooling for confession? The Anglos should have such faith. Anyway, good news. Herlinda will have to complain about her husband's family on another trip.*

But she had another task for him.

"Solo quiero que hable usted con Rosario," *Ok, who was Rosario, I will talk to her.*

"Es que su hermano estaba en ese grupo de muchachos, los que murieron en el desierto," she said. *Arizona, the guys who died because the guy who was taking them to the States dropped them off seventy miles away from the highway. The temperatures in the desert were up to 115 degrees Fahrenheit. Fourteen had died and thirteen had lived. One guy was arrested when he got out of the hospital.*

"Quien es ella?" he asked.

"Aquí está no más," she said

"Que pase ella."

He would see her, of course. She was probably in a state of shock. Had she paid the $1000 for the death trip? That is what it had cost, at least $1000, probably more.

Rosario came into the confessional and then collapsed into the chair.

"Tell the padre everything," said Herlinda, still at the door with her foot keeping it open. *Resourceful.*

Rosario started. It was worse than he might have thought. Her mother had said the brother should stay with her in Mexico. Rosario had convinced her that it was ok. Raul would make it. Then they would send for the mother. They would all be together. Rosario had borrowed the money; her brother was so anxious to try his fortune. He really wanted to get to the States. He wanted to work, to send money to his mother.

"No es tu culpa," he said to the woman. *It is not your fault.*

"People are crazy. When it's their fault, they feel no compunction, and when it is not, they are as guilty as hell," the wisdom of Chairman Jako.

His phone was vibrating, but he kept talking to her. She was weeping copiously; it was as if someone had splashed water on her face. Herlinda knocked at the door and said that they had to go; the young man had to work. He almost said that he thought they had gone already. Laughlin didn't want to look at his watch but could hear the first people for the 4:30 Mass coming in, so it was after four already. *They have to get their seat.*

"So we are praying tonight at the house where we are staying," the woman said, and then paused.

This is where you jump in and tell her that you will be there with bells on.

He began by telling her that he had a Mass with the Neo-Cats. That made no sense to her because she didn't distinguish between movements of the Iglesia Catolica. Well, there was a distinction in types of "misas," he said. It was Mass that was *"muy larga, a veces."* Time was no issue. They would be there all night. They would have food; he could eat there.

"I might not get there till really late," he said. *Because I*

have a homicidal maniac and two crazy lovers dogging my steps,
as well as my friend the ex-priest who is in the hospital, and then
a heavy work schedule on Sunday.

"No importa la hora," said the woman. The hour did
not matter.

He said he would have to write down the address.
No, she had a papelito with the instructions. Herlinda had
provided pen and paper to her.

"I will be there, *pero muy después de las nueve,*" he said
and gently hugged her as he nudged her toward the door.
The organist had stopped playing his prelude piece, the
Mass was about to start. Laughlin looked out the open door
and saw the coast was clear of penitents.

As he walked out of the confessional, Laughlin saw
him.

Chapter Eleven

*Carl," the priest said phlegmatically.

"Father, I need to talk to you," the once and would be future groom said hurriedly.

"I came at midday and I heard you were sick," said Laughlin.

Heard, and smelled that you were sick. Because you puked in the office, Carl Baby. What was that about?

"Where can we talk?"

Oh naturally, let bygones be bygones about the vomit. Let us charge ahead with our agenda.

"I have to help with Mass in a bit. I was going to go to the hospital real quick-like to see a friend."

Was Ronny alright? If I go after the Mass, it could be really late. What if he would die? He'd be the type to come back and haunt you. With his blood pressure so high he could have a stroke or something. And even if he just was resting, Ronny will expect me to come twice. He would probably say I should cancel the Mass.

Carl looked at him with almost bovine tranquillity.

"Ok, let's go to my office."

The crowd at the 4:30 p.m. were generally "seniors." Some of them came to Mass the next day, too. A few of them were looking at Carl in his Bermudas and his polo shirt. *The outfit was probably expensive.* Mary said once that her fiancé had spent more money than she did on clothes.

That should have been a clue that things were not going to work out. I think that was on the first day that the couple had come in for their interview. Something had been happening that day. Oh yeah, the parish picnic. Carl had bought a beer while walking through the food stands and Mary had been upset. He had spent fifteen minutes telling them it did not matter to him. But it was a jerky thing to do, buy a beer before you talk to the priest, and chug it down in front of him. *In the office!*

In the parking lot, the two walked in silence. The priest took great strides and the other almost skipped to keep up. The old people coming to Mass observed them with undisguised curiosity. *"We Catholics are a curious people,"* *Ronny always said.*

"Ok, here we are," said the priest when they entered his office. He noticed that someone had renewed the Glade in the atmosphere.

"I got a plan, but I need your help," said Carl.

"What is the plan?" asked the priest in a neutral tone.

"I want to talk to Mary, but here, with you."

"Why?"

"Why? Father, I have just been screwed for life. I think I have a right to talk to the person who has done it."

"Well, I don't know if it is a right," said the priest.

"Padre, you know I am right on this. I have lost five thousand dollars on this thing, for starters. Not to mention my self-respect. All my friends say the same thing. This is a humiliation. It would have been better to go through with it and then get a divorce, once we sent the thank-you cards."

"Why would you want to make a vow that you knew you were not going to keep? I could never have accepted taking part in something like that," the priest said in a serious tone. *What a piece of work this guy is! Maybe if he could just see another angle of this thing, he can break out of his self-centered attitude.*

"That would have been something between Mare and

me. Besides, being married to me, she would forget that dip. Which will happen sooner or later."

So you might as well make it sooner. Now, another element to the thing. He thinks he can still win her back.

"I think you should not go there," said Laughlin. *Go there. Why do I use such clichéd language when I am talking about serious stuff?*

"I would just like to talk to her. That is all I am asking. That we have a meeting. Half an hour — I don't think that is much to ask considering what she has done to me."

Why had she let the thing go so long? Didn't she wonder whether she might not be better off marrying? Sometimes Laughlin thought that she felt sorry for George. He had been alone; she was a caring person. Then Carl had mocked the other so much when she had brought him along to Thanksgiving dinner with her family. George was a nerd, but maybe even then he thought he would win the race by being slow and steady, like the tortoise and the hare. But Carl had decided to tell her family that they would marry. *Maybe unconsciously, the jerk had sensed something coming. He would cut George off at the pass, another cliché.* So he says to her folks, "I know that I don't deserve her, but I ask her hand in marriage." *He must have seen that in some movie, or maybe somebody told him about it.* It had disarmed everybody, including Mary. They had planned the announcement for Christmas, and he jumped the gun by one month. On Friday after Thanksgiving he had bought her the engagement ring. What had happened to the engagement ring? He supposed Mary had returned it.

"The thing I don't understand is that she is still wearing the ring," said Carl. *What, can he read my thoughts?*

"What do you mean?" the priest asked.

"A friend of mine saw her the other day. Mare was still wearing the engagement ring."

So that other people would not ask her questions? Mary has been *very bad about this whole thing. She should have returned the ring.*

"That is strange," said Laughlin. *Might as well be honest. It's weird. With the people involved in this case, nothing could be ruled out.*

His cell phone hummed again. He saw that it was his sister, frowned, and answered it.

"Hello, Helen," he said.

"How come you always know who is calling?"

"Because the phone has a memory. Well, so do I, and would recognize your number. Why are you upset? Do you always want an element of surprise?"

He is looking at me as though this could be his ex-fiancée, or as Jako puts it, "ex-financing."

The priest looked at Carl and mouthed the words, "My sister." The other nodded gravely. *Why do crazy people have moments that are totally normal? And why do I feel I have to explain anything to him?*

"Billy, I want to know why you haven't called Ma?' said Helen.

Haven't called her? Are we talking one-way street now?

"I thought you were going to call," he said.

I'm not going to sound like a neglectful in front of this groom. "So the priest doesn't call his mother."

"Do you even use the phone? I told Ma you probably have it in your sock drawer."

"You're talking to me on it as we speak. It is right in my hand, dearie. I am in my office, but I have someone with me. Can I call you later? Is Ma going to be with you?"

"That is why I am calling. You know her birthday is next week. Can you come in?"

"I hadn't really thought about it."

"Well, you should, she is going to be seventy-five. We're going to have a party for her and the ladies from crafts, and the ones from the book club are going to be there. They would all love to see you."

"Are you trying to scare me?"

She laughed. *What should I tell her? I could drive in one day, leaving after Mass in the morning. The next day the party, the same day the drive back. That was doable, although it was going to be tiring. Now if Ronald weren't so crazy, he could drive with me. But he would probably think J. Edgar Hoover was on his trail.*

"What day is it? I mean, day of the week; I know the date. I will have to ask my pastor. By the way, Ronny is up here, came to see me but got sick at lunch and I have him in the hospital."

That has certainly taken her off the scent. She really cares about Ronny. For her, Ron is just the funny guy from the seminary. She never had to put up with the countless disappointments that came from believing he would fulfil his commitments. Carl Sand was looking crazy again. *He acts as if he is the soul of patience because he is waiting for me to finish the phone call. That goofy smile.*

"Ok, I better go. I will ask my pastor tonight, if I see him. If not, tomorrow. I don't think there will be a problem. Father Peter will say the extra Masses. The Filipino guy. Thanks. I am glad we are having something. God bless."

The priest looked up at Carl Sand. Again, he looked peculiar. *All I need is the guy to go bonkers on me.*

"Ok, we were talking about you and Mary talking together some time."

"No, not *sometime* —today. It has to be today, any time before midnight, although I would prefer earlier."

"Maybe today is not the day for it," said the priest cautiously.

"It is the day for it. You said once that all we would need is you, two witnesses and us for a wedding."

"I said that when we were discussing the wedding plans. But now…"

"It is still true, isn't it? All you need is to have the two witnesses and we say our vows. We have the license."

Ok, I see. He has gone round the bend!

"You don't think that she is going to go through with it today?"

"Technically, it is feasible, isn't it? I mean, it is legally possible, right?"

"I don't think so. She cancelled the wedding. Why would she change her mind?"

"Father, you don't know her like I do. This whole thing is like some kind of nightmare. I just want to talk to her."

"I am sure that it's a nightmare."

His phone was going off again. It was identified as from the hospital. Again he made a face as if he had no other choice and answered. *This jerk is not going anywhere anyhow.* It was a nurse from the hospital.

"There is a Mr. Ronald Avery here. He says that he is your friend."

"Yes?"

"He wanted to know if you remembered he was alive," said the nurse, and then she giggled. Laughlin heard the deep laugh of his friend somewhere in the background.

"I was with him in the Emergency Room," said Laughlin. "But I had confessions."

"He had confessions," he heard the nurse repeat.

"Then I have Mass for the Neo-Catechumens," he said. *This is stupid to play relay, and I have enough craziness with a madman in my office who thinks he is going to pull off the wedding of the year.*

"He has a Mass for Neon Cumidins," said the nurse.

Laughlin could hear more laughter. *At least Ronny is enjoying himself.*

"I said, 'Neo-Catechumens'"

"He said the Neon thing again," said the nurse.

There was a noise and then he heard Ron's voice.

"Are you having Mass for the Klingons?"

"I said very clearly, 'Neo-Catechumens'," said Laughlin.

"They said you could take me home," said Ronny.

Another noise as the phone changed hands.

"No, sir, that is not the case. He is not in any condition to leave. However, maybe a visit would be in order."

"Right now I have someone with me," he said. "Then I have Mass. Please tell Mr. Avery I will be there after Mass."

He hung up.

"I have a friend in the hospital. We went out to lunch and then his sugar shot up. He was incoherent. I left him in emergency. Now he has a bed, but wants to get out."

Carl looked at the priest as if waiting for more information.

In other words, you aren't the only loco I am dealing with today, do you get my drift? Sometimes I wish I could just say it all at once.

"Well, I'll be back at eight," said Sand suddenly. "Then we can have our talk with Mary."

"I don't know how you can expect me to produce Mary the moment you want to talk to her. That is the hour of the Mass I was just speaking about. And it's a very long Mass in Spanish. What happened was very unfortunate, I'll give you that. I'm sorry. But you have known that for two weeks. Now you have to work out the rest of your lives. I am not involved personally in this thing, I mean, between you two as persons, the personal nature of your whatever you would call this, estrangement?" *You glib S.O.B.* "I mean, of course, I would want you two to reconcile in some way, and that might even include a complete restoration of your relationship." *Liar!* "But I cannot force someone..."

Laughlin's cell went off again. It was Mary. He answered it, but stood up so that *the bridegroom from hell* could not see the name on the screen.

"I'm sorry, are you busy, Padre? George and I would like to talk to you tonight, any hour, it is so urgent."

"Please tell the patient that I will get there after my Mass," Laughlin said. "I cannot talk this minute. No, I will call you back."

"Father, this is Mary, from the wedding which wasn't today," *She doesn't know how close she is to an ambush.*

"My Mass is over about 9:30, and then I am going to the hospital."

But I also have the rosary at that time! I can't forget that.

As I was saying, you could come, but I could never promise I will be able to get Mary to come. Why would I insist on her coming today? What if she wanted George to come?" *Where did that come from? You're on the wire without a net.*

Carl looked at the priest steadily and said, "That would be better yet, Padre. Don't you see it? It is about the three of us, the three of us should talk."

Mary calls me "padre" too—something in the atmosphere? What I can't get over is the look of triumph on his face. His unshaven face, he must be part werewolf the way his five o'clock shadow comes across his face. "Hirsute dude" Ronny would call him. Even his fingers had hairs on them past the second joint. And his eyebrows just a touch from being coalescent. He must be awash in testosterone. Probably be bald by the time he is thirty-five.

"It doesn't seem practical to me. I suggest you call Mary. I will accept to be present but not today."

"Padre, you're involved. That is your job to be involved." Carl was more than content with himself for this observation. He had his keys in his hands and he made a move with his hairy wrist as if he had not a care in the world. "See you later, Padre Bill—or should I say William-o?"

Was that a take-off on Guillermo? Had he heard some of the

"Spanish" talking about me?

"We cannot meet tonight. Not tonight. I'm telling you Carl. I cannot do it. My friend is in very serious condition. Someday next week, when things have blown over, we can try to do something. I'm not promising you anything about Mary, however," said Laughlin.

Maybe the guys were right about not going by your first name. Some priests went by their last name. 'See you later, Padre Bill,' was too familiar. The jerk thinks I am going to have a Camp David meeting between the two and he is going to win.

Chapter Twelve

It was already 5:00 p.m. He did not have much time because he would have to run over to the church in ten minutes to help with the distribution of Holy Communion. He went up to his room and into the bathroom. Almost as soon as he sat down on the toilet his cell went off.

"Hello, Mary," he said.

"Father, did something just happen to you? I called and you talked to me about something else, as if you did not recognize me. Did the calls cross or something?"

"I was with Carl when you called. I didn't want him to know that you were talking to me. He wants to see you in my office at 8:00 tonight. I have a Mass at that time, anyway."

"Oh no, he's taking this hard."

Marvellous power of deduction. Like, we are surprised?

"I guess you could say that. He appeared in the morning and had had a few. I wasn't here, but he threw up all over the office."

"He really can't hold his liquor, for as much as he pretends to be so macho."

That strikes me as a strange response. She is still interpreting him to others.

"Uh-huh."

"George and I would really like to talk to you."

"Carl invited George, too," said Laughlin. *You couldn't make this up to be more absurd.*

"Father, Carl wants to run him over! No, he is just trying to manipulate us. He asked me last week to marry him, so that we wouldn't lose our deposit money for the honeymoon in Hawaii. Like, I am going to get married just to go to Hawaii."

Don't talk to me about how illogical he is. You were going to marry him.

"He said he was trying to call you. I told him that it was impossible to talk to you and me this evening. I have the Neo-Catechumen Mass at eight and then I have to visit a friend in the hospital. The Mass isn't over until nine-thirty, by the time everything gets cleaned up. Then I have to go to the hospital. Plus, there is a rosary in Spanish at a house."

I'm making excuses to get out of an unreasonable demand. Why do I do this? I'm entering their absurd world and I sound absurd. There is a Scripture about talking to a fool in his folly.

"I'm glad you told him that you couldn't see him again today. But you haven't seen us. Let's do this. You're going to the hospital. We will talk at the hospital. They must have a coffee shop. Before or after your visit, when you are ready. We can meet in the lobby. It is Trinitas where your friend is---right?"

"Yes." Why in the hell are you telling her this?

"We will see you just for a minute."

"I really don't want to."

"Father, we need you. It will be five minutes. In the parking lot, if need be."

"Don't count on it. There are other things going on. I don't know how my friend is doing."

"We'll pray for him, Father."

"Pray for Carl." *And you bring him up… because?*

"He goes gonzo, I know. He looks like he's retarded when he does that. Ok, take it easy, Padre. I am worried about Carl, too. I hope he doesn't get suicidal."

You're kidding me, right? You want to set my mind at ease and you tell me that you hope he is not suicidal when the reason he might be is because you dumped him with two weeks before the wedding.

"I really…" The intercom phone was ringing.

"I'll let you go until later, Padre."

Marilu was on the phone.

"There is a Spanish lady here to see you. Her name is Rosario."

Rosario. Rosario. The name was attached to something I heard today.

"Send her over to the house, Marilu."

"Are you sure? Father Jako is just finishing up the financial report."

"Really? But it's five-ten."

"It's a long report this year."

"So I have about ten minutes before Father rips through the Mass prayers."

"Father, you're too funny. I would rather not send the lady over."

"What is the alternative?"

"You could come over here and set up an appointment. I think a car is waiting for her."

"I'll be right over, tell her."

When he saw her, she immediately broke into sobs. He remembered now. Rosario was the one who lost her brother in the Arizona desert.

"Padre queremos que venga a la casa a rezar con nosotros."

"Ya dije que si!" *I should have said, "I am sorry I even said I would go." Translating thoughts makes for choppy communication.*

"Hemos pedido que venga una rezadora también."

Rezadora? Then technically you don't need me. She will say the rosary with you.

"Ella puede empezar el rosario mientras yo pudiera estar en camino. Porque, como le dije, tengo que celebrar la misa," he said. *I'm sounding like a gavacho from a movie. It happens when I start translating thoughts. She can start and finish the whole thing, for all I care this evening. Again, choppy. I should've asked again when and where and then said something about the Mass, maybe even tell about Ronny.*

"Sabemos, Padre," she said. *We know. That means you have to do a hell or high-water thing.*

"Pero no puedo hasta muy tarde," he said. *You should have said, "No puedo"; how can you say that you will be there late with all that is going on?*

"Gracias, Padre. Y hoy quiero saber si puedo prestar un crucifijo y unas velas."

So that is why she had to see me again. She needs to borrow a crucifix. Which one can I give her? There is one in the office. And candles. I can get those in the sacristy. Marilu is a pushover for that stuff. Jako might expect payment, especially today with the financial report going on.

"Voy a ver lo que podemos prestar," he said. Then he told Marilu to get the candles. Before she came back Rosario insisted he write down her address.

Marilu looked suspiciously at him as he asked for pen and paper to write down the address. *I could go to the hospital at any time, 10 or even 11. This will get me out of the meeting with Mary and George and/or Carl. What a relief, finding work consoling people for a tragedy instead of participating in another.*

"Marilu, is this Mass crowded?"

"No, for some reason, there is a light crowd."

Fr. Peter was in the yard when Laughlin crossed it to go to the rectory.

"Peter, there are few people in Mass. Do you think you guys could do without me? Ron is in the hospital, I had to leave him in the emergency room and I want to check on him before Mass."

"No problem. Tell Avery my prayers."

Laughlin went into the rectory and looked around the waiting room. There was a blond wood Jesus hanging on the cross, finely carved. It looked European. He told Rosario that she had to give it back tomorrow or he would be in trouble. She cried, kissed the image and said she would guard it like an only child. Nobody ordinarily came to the office on weekends so the priests would probably not notice the crucifix missing.

He got into his car and drove away.

Chapter Thirteen

In the hospital, he climbed the stairs instead of going to the elevator. It was his only exercise, and it was quicker. Occasionally, he met other people on the stairs, and always felt as though he were doing something wrong. He would tell them, "I'm making the rounds," in case they thought he loved to hang out in the stairwells.

"Hello, Ronald Avery, Jr.," Laughlin said as he entered his friend's room.

"William, you are here at last," said Ronny, "Take me home."

"I can't take you home, Ronny. They have to run the tests and figure out what happened. You aren't ready to go home."

"William, tell me something. You are my friend, is that correct? Friends don't leave friends abandoned in the hospital."

"You got to be kidding, Ronny. I did not abandon you. I had to go do confessions. Look at me, I'm here right now."

"I don't know what has happened to our friendship. Once I thought you were so loyal."

"What are you talking about?"

"You have been ignoring me lately. I always have to take the initiative. You're always busy. Here I am, all by my lonesome in this awful hospital."

"It's not awful, come on. You're going to be all right.

These things happen. They're signs."

"Oh, aren't you taking this spiritually?"

"Chill, Ronny. Take it easy."

"How am I supposed to be taking it easy when you are looking at your watch?"

"I have got a Mass at eight."

"At eight. That is three hours from now."

"Two and a half hours from now. However, there is a Mass right now and my pastor expects me to be there for Communion. And I can't just walk in at five to eight to the other Mass. There are people to attend to, issues."

"See what I mean? I can be dying and you are running off to another Mass. You're looking at someone who wants to talk to you."

"But you're not dying, and I will be back after Mass in the evening," Laughlin said.

He didn't hear that a hospital worker had entered behind him, because he was trying to calculate the moment to leave and was anxious to be down the stairs.

"I know I'm not dying, I shouldn't even be here," said Ronny.

"Ok, let's talk about that later. Are you cooled down? I don't know what kind of mood you're in, you keep blaming me. Next thing I know, you'll be singing me, 'You don't bring me flowers anymore.'"

At this, the orderly laughed. She was a short woman, with hair the color people say is like dishwater, a little overweight. Her head and face seemed large for her body, and she had burst into laughter. She was very fair and so her face reddened with her amusement. So did Laughlin's.

Of course, Ronny enjoyed the laughter. He began to sing the song, which left the woman in an almost ecstatic state.

"Will you watch him while I'm at Mass?" Laughlin asked her, "He's not going to be your evening's easiest patient."

"But he's the most entertaining, that's for sure. I wanted to know about diet restrictions or preferences, we are late on serving dinner, some problem downstairs."

The woman has a good sense of humor, a plus, dealing with Ronny.

"Ronny, I got to go, I'll see you."

Jako will want to know where I am. This is a good moment to get away, because he has another audience.

He hurried down the stairs, missing the first floor exit and ended up in the basement. So this was the kitchen. It looked old, like the kitchen of the old seminary.

He had startled two young men who were working in the kitchen, their white uniforms contrasting with their brown skin.

"Disculpen," he said automatically. The skin color and their faces made him presume they spoke Spanish, but this had been an unconscious process.

"Padre!" one of them said.

"Si?"

"Voy a la misa a su iglesia."

Of course I didn't recognize one of the flock when it counts.

He asked them some questions. The one who talked the most was named Rodrigo. How long were they working there? He told them that a friend of his was in the hospital, even that he had taken him to the restaurant, because they would know the place.

They are pleased seeing me, feeling that they can show me something. They don't seem to mind that I have got in here by mistake. One flight of stairs too many. It's hard being a genius.

The other one, not Rodrigo, walked him up the stairs to the exit to the lobby. He asked him his name.

"Sergio," he said, "para servirle."

"At your service." The only really polite people these days are the campesinos.

Outside the doors of the hospital he began to trot to his car. It was now six-fifteen and Jako was giving a long report. That meant he could still help with communions at the six o'clock.

In the car he thought he should call Ron's mother. What if anything happened and she might be waiting for him?

"Hello, Mrs. Avery, this is Bill," he said when she answered.

"God answers prayers. I was just hunting down your number. How y'all doin'? I need to talk to you."

"Me too. Ronny is up here in Zachary with me."

"He is? That Chile is going to be the death of me, I tell you, Beel, he been real bad lately."

"His health is no good. I had to take him to the hospital because his sugar is high."

"We didn't know where he was. At least he is with you."

"But he's in the hospital."

"What?"

It didn't register the first time I said it.

"He's in Trinitas Hospital here."

"Which hospital?"

"Trinitas."

"Trinity?"

"Yeah."

"How did he get there?"

"We were having lunch and he got incoherent."

"What he get?"

"He started talking crazy. And he was like confused."

"That sounds like him. That's from his father's side of the family. Strange people."

"No, I mean worse than usual. They were following him. He was getting paranoid."

"He's been getting paranoid around us too."

"We went to the Emergency Room. His sugar was up

past 400."

"Oh, Beel. God sent you to us. What would Ronny do without you?"

"He wouldn't have gone to the Emergency Room, because I had to fight him."

"And what about that boy Reginald? Was he over there by you?"

"Who's Reginald?"

"That is what we've been wondering. Besides bad company. I think he helped Ronny lose the Dry Cleaning business."

"Ronny lost the Dry Cleaning business?"

"Sure did. That boy has no head for business. First the video place and then the Dry Cleaning. I think Reginald stole some money from Ron. Because he is broke, with a capital 'B.' We haven't seen him for a week, since they closed the place up. His brother thought he saw Reginald out somewhere, but alone. That boy's using crack or sommit."

"Ronny didn't tell me anything."

"Well, 'cause you is family. He never tells nothin' to family. Ask him about it. And about that boy Reginald. A white boy, skinny thing. Real skinny. Nanny Ruth first one think maybe that boy is taking drugs."

The plot thickens. So this is Ronny's new crisis. No wonder he looked me up. Every time things go to Scheiss *for him he remembers me.*

"Mrs. Avery, I gotta go now. I will call you later when I'm with Ronny. Right now I have services."

"Ok, say your Mass, honey. I'll talk to you later."

I said services thinking she wouldn't know the word "Mass". But of course she knows. Who is this Reginald? Doesn't even sound like a white boy name to me. Another of Ronny's "close friends"? Where did he pick him up?

He was leaving the hospital when he heard his name

called.

"Father Laughlin, Father Laughlin."

He could not immediately identify the young man was raced up to him.

"Father Laughlin, Ray Horvath."

"Of course, Mary's brother."

"What are you doing here, Father?"

"A friend of mine is visiting. We went out to lunch and he got very sick. I had to take him to Emergency. He has had a problem with diabetes. It flared up."

"That's what Mary said. She told me I might find you here."

"You mean, the reason you are here is to meet me?"

"Exactly. I didn't tell Mary, but I have some serious concern for her. Carl Sand wants to kill George."

"Mary told me."

"She doesn't know how serious it is. Sand is a hunter. He knows how to use guns."

"He's still in love with your sister."

Great comment, Laughlin. That is really enlightening. No flies on you.

"If you call it that, Father. Carl was doing something fishy with Joyce Collins."

Which doesn't surprise me, but I can't say that.

"I saw them do something at a party. By accident. I had gone looking for a bathroom and there was a suite. Long-story-short I discovered them kissing. This was like the middle of May."

"And you told your sister?"

"Can we sit down somewhere?"

They found a couch near some plants in the lobby. *I'll miss Communion, again.*

"I didn't tell my sister because Carl knew something about me."

"In other words, he knew you saw him with Joyce, but

he had some information against you that made you keep silent. He blackmailed you?"

"Yes. Well, he said that Joyce was just a party girl and it was like a fling. He said he knew worse about me."

"And he did?"

"Yes."

"And it was so bad that you decided not to tell Mary that her so-called best friend was playing around with her husband-to-be?"

"Father, Carl Sand knew that I had done something illegal."

"Something criminal?"

"No, well, yeah. But that was not the most important part. Right after Easter, we went down to the Sand beach house near Cape May. I took a friend from college and a buddy from high school met us there. Some of Carl's buddies were going to go to the beach but bailed out the last minute. So we went with Carl, but he was late because he had to see a client about a car on a Friday night. He came very late, but just in time to find out what we were doing."

"Did you steal something?"

"Oh, no."

"Were you using drugs?"

"Yes, I guess I might as well tell you. We got a buzz going and went down to the beach at night. I guess someone called the cops, they must have smelled the weed."

"So the police arrested you?"

"No, we fled. They did get this other guy who was with us because he was in no shape to run. We weren't either, but somehow we evaded the cops."

"And Carl saw you guys?"

"We had been swimming and hadn't time to dress when we had to run."

"So, it was a beach, you were in your trunks."

"Actually, we had been skinny-dipping. We were high

and it seemed like a good idea."

Of course.

"After I saw him and Joyce, Carl texted me a message. 'dirt on me, dirt on you, she's a slut, and would do it with anybody but you are a ---.'"

"So you kept silent. But Mary knew you hated him."

"Because I showed that but couldn't tell why. Now Joyce tells me that Sand wants to bring us all down. He is going to broadcast I am a pot-head. My father is going to kill me."

"And then you can tell everyone he needs to prove it. Besides the fact that you can say that Joyce was moving in on Mary. It turns the tables, making it look like Mary knew something."

What would Jako say? I don't have to be involved in their problems.

"You don't know my mother and father."

"I've met them."

"Yes, at church. You can't know what their reaction would be."

"What cannot be avoided must be accepted." *Sententiousness instead of sympathy. Shame on you.*

Ray was silent for a moment. His face showed tension because his jaw was taught and his lips pursed up.

"Father, it is a little more involved. I took something from their beach house."

"You mean you stole something? I thought you said you didn't steal anything. What was it? Why would you do something like that?"

"Well, it was my friend's idea. It was more like borrowing. It was my buddy from high school. He said that he was going to get some money and buy it back from the guy who sold us the weed."

"Buy what back?"

"It was like borrowing it. We thought we could replace

it later. It was a gold chain that Carl's mother had left there."

"You stole a gold chain from the beach house?"

"We were trying some other stuff."

"Other stuff?"

"It was crack."

"You were smoking crack? Has that continued?"

"It was the first and last time. No, well, once more. I think Carl guessed because we were really high when we came in."

"Without your clothes from the beach? In April?"

"Originally we were going to have a bonfire. But then we thought it would be fun to have a swim. Just when we were ready the cops came. But it wasn't just weed, either. We started with weed and then this guy whom my buddy knew said he had some other stuff. He's the one that got caught, fat guy and he couldn't run. I didn't know my buddy had set it up. That is why he had borrowed the chain. He takes it out and I'm like, where is that from? He had changed in the Sand's master bedroom. It was like pawning it. He hadn't had time to go to the ATM."

"You're lucky the dealer didn't try to turn you guys in."

"He had his own deal going. His uncle was a big backer of the senator."

That helps.

"So anyway, we just took a couple of puffs and then my buddy saw the policemen because they had flashlights on the beach. The police got the crack, too, so if we had been arrested we would have got charges."

The priest looked at his watch. It was 6:30, so he was definitely missing the communion. Where was this going?

"You're afraid that Carl is going to tell the police about the crack?"

"No, there would be no proof. I mean, the thing didn't even make the local paper. The necklace is what we never recovered. The police got it. Carl has to claim it and to do so would mean…well, it would be complicated. They would probably want him to press charges or something."

"Explaining how it went missing. But he would have no proof."

"Just that we told him about it. And promised to get it back."

"But you didn't. And the police still have it?"

"He went to the station to get it but they said he had to make a report. He was also drunk at the time, so they told him to come back, which he never did."

"So you think that he might tell your parents."

"Yeah. It was just a thin gold chain with this little shell."

"Can't you replace it? Why did you tell Carl."

"I was yelling at Jim, my buddy and Carl overheard me. He accused us of stealing more stuff--some rings. We admitted about the chain."

"So maybe you should confess to Mrs. Sand?"

"Coming on top of the cancelled wedding, they might get us in trouble."

"You're right, it's a mess. But let me understand this. Why are you telling me this now?"

"Mary and I had a fight this week. Our father was yelling at her and she threw me under the bus. But I also think that I should tell Mary about Joyce, because Mare feels so guilty, but am afraid that she will say something to him and open the whole garbage can."

I think you were looking for the expression "open a can of worms." So, you have friends who steal from people's beach houses or "borrow." Then you get in trouble on a cold night in April smoking pot and skinny dipping. And the dealer has good connections but the police have the "almost like pawned" necklace. Ok, and where do we go from here?

"What do you want me to do?"

"I'm just telling you this because Joyce says Carl wants to go through with it."

"Through with what?"

"The wedding. I don't think you should let them get married."

"That is not an option right now."

"Ok, but I'm telling you. Carl is crazy, I mean, really nuts."

He does have a point there.

"Ok, I'll have to remember that."

Chapter Fourteen

The garage was attached to the rectory. There were four spaces for cars, but each priest had only one car, so the last space had the lawn mower, some tires that looked almost new, supposedly Stashu's, and a bicycle that Fr. Jako had bought on a whim but never had used. The remote caused the door to open for Laughlin, but at a slower pace than he expected, which meant he almost hit the ascending door with the roof of the car.

Of course he had missed distributing communion at the six o'clock Mass. He would have to tell Jako about the hospital. *Maybe I can play up how sick Ronny is.*

He walked down the corridor that led to the kitchen and heard an animated conversation going on in Filipino-accented English. A woman's voice stood out and what she said must have been funny, because her remarks were punctuated by laughter.

As he entered, the group fell silent. The only one he knew was Gloria Macau—or something like that, it seemed ridiculous to have a surname like the bird—a regular visitor of Fr. Peter. Jako called her the Black Widow, because she had been married to two Filipino military men, both generals, and had seemed to prosper with matrimony. "She, ah, she has lots of money," Father Peter had told Bill once. Jako had said, "Probably stolen." Fr. Peter had said, "No, her last husband, he fought against Marcos." Jako had replied, "No honor among thieves." Jako was capable of the most outrageous comments, and yet seemed to think he was the essence of a gentleman.

Whatever Gloria had been talking about must not have been for the tender ears of forty-year-old priests, because she had just stopped talking.

"Having a party?" asked Laughlin.

Fr. Peter seemed relieved at the question. *Sometimes the most anodyne remarks can save the day by cutting the proverbial* hielo.

"Yes, today is St. John the Baptist. Gloria comes from a town where it's a big feast day."

"*Felicidades,*" he said automatically. He always wanted to speak Spanish to Filipinos. *Echoes of the Spanish Empire in my head?*

"All good special food for saint," said Fr. Peter. "This kitchen is close to heaven."

This kind of stuff makes him happy. This works for him. For someone who hardly eats, he is waxing eloquent.

"Father, you want some of my cooking?" asked Gloria.

"I have Mass in a little bit," he said, "Maybe you can save some."

He looked at the bowls of food on the table.

What would Jako say about this? He knew what he would say, "Probably some kid's pet was thrown into the soup. *Spot soufflé,* or *filet Fido.*" He had some set jokes, and that was his line about Filipino food. "They eat dog meat," he had said once almost within hearing of a group of priests who had come to visit Peter.

"We also celebrating new marriage for Gloria," said a lady, who looked younger than Gloria. "She will marry Mr. Sin."

An older gentleman cleared his throat. He looked very Chinese, *which was natural with a name that Sin. Wasn't there a Cardinal Sin? Yes, I am sure there was, not like the novel, however,* Cardinal Sins. *The Reverend Andrew Greeley was like a smart bratty kid acting out when he wrote that trash.*

"Congratulations," said Laughlin very seriously.

"You have a big mouth, Lulu," said Gloria, but she was laughing.

"Ok, we not celebrating engagement. We celebrating ceasefire with Abu Sayyaf," Lulu said.

This did not go over well with the rest of the group, which was comprised of Fr. Peter, Gloria, Mr. Sin, a man who might be connected to this last, and a good friend of Gloria whose name Laughlin could not remember, *maybe Dolores?*

"What is that?" asked the priest.

"Some Muslims in Mindanao. Ghadafy has made peace talks, ceasefire," said Father Peter.

"Oh, I see," said Laughlin. *Why are they all looking at me like that?* "Did you say Ghadafy—from Libya?"

"Yes, Ghadafy. He is now interfering in Philippines," said Lulu.

"They are not Abu Sayyaf," said Mr. Sin in a calm voice. "That is joke. No negotiation with terrorists. Not even Moro Islamic Liberation Front."

"I forgot about the fighting over there," said Laughlin. *Brilliant way to make friends, Bill, telling them that their country is just not on your map of the world.*

"It is very bad," said Gloria. "Yesterday they find three soldiers with their heads cut off." She made a gesture with her finger crossing her throat.

This parish is as big as the world, he thought. It was a line an Italian nun had repeated to him many times in the missions. Her parish in Italy had had a great sense of mission. *In this corner of New Jersey, we are talking about some people on the other side of the globe. Jako would probably mock us for it. "What ever happened to 'bloom where you are planted?'" he told me once. Let's face it--- the guy is strange.*

"I have got to run to get ready for Mass," he said, but he remembered to smile. *When you smile you can get away with anything. Who said that? Now I know why some people write things down. I used to remember everything I wanted to recall, practically speaking.*

Father Peter suddenly looked serious, "Father Louis Bertrand, he's looking for you."

"He is?"

Now the reckoning. Could he really be angry I missed giving communion?

He ran up the stairs. Jako had put the elevator in when the old monsignor was still around but had not used it the first few years. *Probably because he thought each ride cost money.* Jako had been the old priest's servant, for all intents and purposes, he had been sent by the bishop to take care of a revered and cantankerous priest. *In the old days, there was no such thing as retirement.*

Laughlin was a little tired this evening, and felt winded on the steps. *I have got to do something about my avoirdupois. Just out of shape.* He stopped in his room. On his way to the bathroom he looked at his bed. *I wouldn't mind diving into it for a few hours,* he thought. *This day has been nuts, and it is bound to get nuttier if Carl Sands has his way.*

His cell phone started humming again when he was urinating in the toilet. He answered and then was afraid that his evacuation might be too loud. Aiming at the side of the toilet bowl was easier thought of than accomplished with one hand holding the phone.

It was his sister. *She always knows when to call.*

"Well, have you talked to Mom yet today?"

"As you know, of course, not yet, but you won't believe what has happened to me today."

"When was the last time you talked to your mother?"

"She is still your mother, too, no?"

"I call her or see her every day."

You don't live in New Jersey. You don't have people like Priscilla Bidener stalking you, nor weddings that are called off at the last minute nor a friend like Ron Avery. You don't have to live in a house that is like a fire station, with two priests who could be subjects of case studies.

"How is she doing?"

"She misses you."

Uh-oh. Are we going to do the whole "Come back, Little Sheba" thing, or what?

"I miss both of you. This place is a little crazy. We had a couple cancel a wedding with less than two weeks. It was supposed to be today, and the ex-groom is calling me wanting a meeting with the ex- bride to be." *Did I tell her this the last time she called? I can't remember.*

"Don't get too involved with the crazies, Billy, they'll make you nuts, too."

Thanks, honey, but that criterion might severely limit my parish operations here.

"Good concept, we're starting to sound like Franny and Zooey again. You know what, Sis? I'll call you back. The pastor is looking for me and I have to get ready for the Neo-Cats." *And I am hurting myself by restraining my urination.*

"Ok, I'm very sorry to bother you."

"It's not bothering me. It's just work, I have a Mass. And after that I have to go to the hospital because my friend Ron is still in there." *I am sure I told her that.*

"Ron? What is happening to him? Is he coming back?"

That was Helen for you, hoping that Ron would come back. Come back to what? He was certainly not coming back to ministry soon. Was that even possible? Maybe he could end up like one of those old problem priests they talked about, who reconcile with the Church on their deathbed, or they get sick and they put them in a convent saying Mass for cloistered nuns.

"Not right now. At this moment he is plotting to get out of the hospital. His sugar was up to 400, and his blood pressure is through the roof. Oh, and I went to see Sor Margarita today. She sends her love."

"Is she bad?"

"I think terminal," he said, but there was a knock on the door. He heard Jako's voice saying, "Are you there?"

"Father Jako is looking for me. Later, dearie. I love you, kiddo, God bless."

She hesitated and said, "I love you too, I just wish — we will have to talk."

And that is all. She has a flair for exit lines. She should have been in the Parthian cavalry.

"Are you there?" he heard Jako again.

"In a minute. Be right there." *What the hell does he want?*

While he finished his business in the toilet bowl, Bill looked at the bathroom mirror. He had taped onto it the Pioneer Pledge of Total Abstinence and a small card, typed on an index card, a favorite quote from his student days.

> **This is God's universe, buddy, not yours, and he has the final word about what is ego and what's not.**
>
> **Zooey to Franny**

When he opened the door, Jako was looming in the space in front of the door. The weak light of the hallway made it seem like he was even larger than in life.

"Are you ready to go?"

"Go?"

"To grab a bite to eat."

"I've got Mass in an hour. I told the Filipino party I was getting ready for the Neo-Cats."

"You didn't want *filet of Fido*? We'll go to the Tropicana; we'll be in and out. The Spanish start late anyway. You'll be ready before they are. You could eat a ham sandwich in the entrance procession and by communion still have your hour fast."

Laughlin wondered how to say no and not offend the old man.

"Come on, I have to tell you something, anyway, without Fu Manchu poking his chop stick in."

That sealed it. I have to go.

"Ok, I hope it's not crowded."

"We'll be in good shape. I'll meet you at the garage."

He went down to the office, which smelled like another fog of Glade had descended. When he got to the garage, Jako was in the car. As he got in, Jako adjusted the volume of the radio.

"Earthquake in Peru. Just now. CNN has the story. Some kind of tidal wave came and hit the shore. Some kind of Jap name."

"Tsunami?" asked Laughlin.

"That's it. You might tell your people. Might have relatives there."

"The Neo-Cats are mostly Columbians and Cubans," Laughlin said.

"Same neighborhood. You better tell them to pray for their relatives. Monster waves."

There was one like that in Nicaragua when I was near there visiting in El Salvador. But if I try to talk to him about it, he'll get it all wrong. Then I'll have to hear his version of what I said for a few months. It will end up I was there on the beach or something. Between his hearing loss and his idées fixes, it was not easy to have a conversation with Jako.

It was rare that Laughlin had been alone with Jako in his Mercedes and in the front seat. Usually, he let Peter sit in the front when they went out to eat.

"What about your friend?"

"He's ok. I'm going over to the hospital later on." *He must be lonely; he is trying so hard to be conversational. Which does not match my mood.*

"I'm surprised you didn't want to schmooze with Gloria Macau," Laughlin joked.

"Why did you think that?" asked Jako.

"For the cuisine from the Philippines," said Laughlin laughing. "I know you like that kind of food."

"I heard all that racket and escaped up the elevator. That Gloria is *mulier fortis* if there ever was one. *Fortissima*. I heard she has a new beau. The car looks like it is out of the *Godfather* movie. She knows how to snag them. Talk about a Black Widow Spider."

When they were seated at the restaurant, Laughlin remembered how hungry he was. He would have to eat later at the rosary. *I'll order a salad.* Father Jako ordered a burger and fries. When he ordered the salad, Jako looked at him over the frames of his glasses.

"A salad on a Saturday night?"

"I'm trying to cut down," he said.

"What, you want to lose weight?"

"I wouldn't mind."

"You know what the old man said, 'A priest losing weight, you have to ask for whom?'"

The old man was Monsignor Kruppshock, the pastor whom Jako had succeeded.

"I wonder what that wave looked like," Jako said.

"Probably like I feel," said Laughlin.

"What?"

"Nothing, sometimes I feel like a tsunami is heading for me."

"I've told you about that. You need to change the pace. We're in it for the long haul."

The salad was served, much to the mirth of the pastor, who had an enormous hamburger before him, and a heap of French-fried potatoes. They said a hurried grace, something Laughlin always insisted on.

And then Jako dropped the bomb.

"You missed hearing the financial report both Masses."

"I'm sorry; it has been such a crazy day."

"The joker get over his wedding bell blues yet?"

"Why don't you ask him? He just walked in the restaurant?"

The wild-eyed Mr. Sand was waiting to be seated. He was looking frantically around until he saw Laughlin. Clearly disappointed to see him with the older priest, he apparently asked to use the restroom. *Just checking if they're hiding, probably. Like I'm going to rendezvous with George and Mary at the Tropicana?*

"For crying out loud. Did he follow us?" asked Jako.

"Must have. He thinks I am going to being meeting with his ex-fiancée."

"Persistent SOB. Kind of steps on my toes, though, because I have something to tell you."

"He must have been disappointed in the restrooms, he's going out again."

"Like I said, I have to talk to you. The financial report was not that bad. We're in the black, even with the school, which is better than some of our neighbors. The parish is in decent shape. The rectory could use a make-over, but most of the people are good people. There are some crazies, like Priscilla Bidener and whoever this young jerk is who was going to get married today, but we have good people."

"Holy Trinity is a nice parish."

"And you should be looking to the future. You are getting to be a pastor's age. I know that mission thing didn't work out with you getting sick down there."

"St. James Society would have me back, but the bishop won't let me."

"Right. But there is mission right here. The Spanish people like you. The old timers are charmed by your absent-minded professor style. No offense, I'm joking, but they like you even when you're not down-to-earth."

Where is this going?

"The people are nice to me."

"They love you. That is why I told Peter we had to watch you more closely. You could get overconfident, they like you so much. But I think you would make a good pastor."

"But you have four years to go."

"Not anymore. My doctor took it upon himself to call the bishop. He's given me two months to get things straightened away."

"What is your doctor concerned about?"

"It's not the diabetes so much now. My heart is punking out. Then my damned prostate, which has never been any use to me, has decided to go cancerous. I need to take care of these things, he says. When I didn't schedule surgeries, he calls the bishop, the tricky bastard."

"You mean the doctor?" Laughlin said as a joke.

"Ha hah! Not a bad joke, for you. Yeah, I meant the doctor. But the bishop he says, 'Any thoughts on your successor?' If that damned Polack could have kept his eyes from roving, he would have been a great one. But he just got in trouble again. So, I think it's you. As far as I'm concerned, you're the only one who won't ruin the parish."

Heart-warming endorsement.

"But all of this depends on the personnel group recommending someone to the bishop." Laughlin was nervous.

"Yes, but the bishop asked me. He was thinking of one of those Columbian guys, but I said that it was a delicate balance in the parish."

The plot thickens. I am the great white hope for the parish.

"Well, thank you for the vote of confidence. The people will be upset if you retire early."

"Not with a smooth transition."

This is a new side of Jako, the pastoral psychologist.

Laughlin had finished the salad. *I didn't eat lunch, no wonder I'm hungry. But what's with Jako? He hardly touched his fries and he ate only a part of the hamburger. What time is it?*

"Don't worry about the time. We have plenty of time."

"You hardly ate anything," said Laughlin.

"My eyes are too big for my stomach. Haven't had much of an appetite lately. Damned prostate must be too close to my stomach."

Interesting anatomy theory. He really is not feeling well.

There was a moment of silence. The waiter had seen Jako's hand gesture summoning him. The pastor had taken out his roll of cash to pay the check.

"Well, we've got to be going. I really have to think about what we were talking about. I have Mass. Thanks for dinner. I never finished my lunch."

"Because of the Emergency Room visit? I hope your pal is ok."

On their way back, Jako let on a little of the disappointment he had about the bishop's decision.

"In the old days, the pastor would stay but the bishop would send someone who could be the power behind the throne. Now you're out on the street. Well, I have my condo. It's practically ready. I guess I'm ready."

When they pulled in the drive to the church, they saw some Neo-Cats going into the church.

"I'll leave you off here," said Jako. "Your people are waiting."

"Ok, and thanks for the news bulletin."

"What news bulletin?"

"The one about Peru."

"Oh yeah, that's right. At least you ought to have a petition about it."

A rare display of piety. That is something.

Chapter Fifteen

The sacristy was full of people. Laughlin could see a group around the vestment case. The altar boys were playing with the incense. *I am sorry I even started that incense stuff.* The Catechists were waiting for him, too. *That could be complicated. They might have some big idea for the liturgy, and I have to make the Mass short—or rather, la Eucaristia, as they said, or la Liturgia. I have the dead people in Arizona and Ronny and the wedding that wasn't waiting for me.*

Magdalena, one of the regulars, was looking around, too. She obviously wanted to talk. *Probably about Eugenio, her husband. And that is never brief.* Two young men, in dress shirts with ties were going to do the readings. That was a new idea of the Catechists. *Dress your best for the Lord.*

"Listos?" said Laughlin as he walked in.

"Tenemos que hablar," said one of the catechists. Laughlin always mixed the two of them up. One was Pedro and the other was Pablo. They were cousins or something.

"Háblenme," said Laughlin without much enthusiasm.

"In private," said the one who was probably Pablo.

"After Mass?" asked Laughlin.

"Antes. Pero usted debe atender primero a este señor."

Until then, Laughlin had not noticed Carl Sands sitting on the bench by the windows. The once and future would-be groom was smiling. *Here we go.*

"I told you that I was busy with Mass," he said firmly.

"I know. I'll just stay here."

How am I going to get rid of him? He is going to wait here until Mary comes. Why is he dressed like this? He has a tee shirt on that looks clean, and pants that have suspenders. Is he still drunk? He didn't sound so bad, but his idiotic grin might be an indication.

"How about if I open up my office? This Mass usually takes a long time, and people want to see me after."

Of course I know that's a bad idea. Wasn't this the guy who was upchucking in the morning all over the office? Nevertheless, I could stick him in my office and maybe he'll fall asleep. I could maybe call his family. He has a funny color, however. What if he throws up again?

"I don't know," he said. "Has Mare confirmed our tête a tête?" he asked.

Now his tone is friendly about "Mare." Don't get sentimental on me, Carl. He doesn't even look like someone who knows what tête a tête means.

"No, she hasn't. I can answer just for myself. There is a family I have to visit because someone died in Arizona in a tragedy. Then I have a sick friend in the hospital, whom I really need to visit."

This was a bit abrupt, even for him, so he added, "We are going to have to talk some other time. I know this has been a terrible day for you."

"It's not over yet," said Carl.

"That's right," said the priest. Then he reacted, his face looking like someone just hit him. *The pants, they're from the tux. He is wearing his suit pants. His shirt is probably still in the car. Is he thinking he can pull something off? A hunter and the proverbial shotgun wedding? No, he doesn't look so violent. And he is grinning. He doesn't look malicious, just goofy.*

Carl stood up. *I better not put him back in the house alone,* thought Laughlin.

"You know, Carl, why don't you just hang out here during the Mass? It's long, but we will talk afterward. Briefly, that is, because I have to get a few things done before midnight." *Miles to go before I sleep, bucko.*

"Cool," said Carl. *Could he still be drunk? There he goes again with the grin. Wait until Ronny hears about this one. He will die laughing. Well, probably there is a better word than to use than dying, under the circumstances. What if Ronny is really seriously ill? I have to get him to call his family.*

"Let's get this show on the road," said the priest. No one but Carl understood the idiom. "Que el Señor nos bendiga en esta santa eucaristía, en el nombre del Padre y del Hijo y del Espíritu Santo." *That they understood.*

"Pero Padre, necesitamos hablar."

Oh yeah, I forgot.

"Si, como no," he said.

"En privado."

He took them over to the other side of the sacristy, the part that had once been called the "boys" sacristy or the "servers" sacristy.

"Ok, diganme," he said.

They were concerned about the way the *Eucaristia* was going. What did that mean? They felt that there were people who might not really understand what was taking place. For that reason, there had to be instruction for the people to understand what they were engaged in.

"Quieren que les preparo algo?"

No, it wasn't that he had to do it. In fact, it had already been done. The problem was that the people who were prepared knew what they were doing. The visitors did not. Who were the visitors? The persons who had not been invited or prepared.

Did they mean the man he had just talked with over there? Maybe they should know that the man was suffering from the greatest disappointment of his life. His bride-to-be had cancelled the wedding. The man was crazy with grief. The two men looked at each other and there was no way of knowing whether they thought much of the story. Anyway, no, they didn't mean the man in the suspenders. They meant others who were slipping in the church during the inappropriate times. How could they understand the sharing about the Word? It was a disservice to them to allow them to come in. They could actually be turned against the *Camino* because they might be bored. They needed milk and then meat was fed to them.

Of course they could not neglect to mention that they were in possession of special knowledge. The Camino *has a clubby kind of Gnosticism as a consolation for all that discipline. We need meat and the others are still on milk.*

It was time to start the *Eucaristia,* he said. What was the solution to this issue of visitors? They were very pleased that he had asked that question.

"We must lock the doors during our Eucharist. That way no one will stray in who shouldn't."

"When do you want to start locking the doors?" Laughlin was too tired to argue.

"Tonight. No time like the present," said one of them, maybe it was Pablo.

"I will have to talk with the pastor," the priest said.

"Couldn't we try it tonight and then talk to the pastor?" This was not the one who might be Pablo, hence Pedro.

You guys always have to have it your way. I am not in any mood to fight.

"Ok, *ad experimentum,*" he said.

They nodded, but he doubted they knew what he was saying. He gave them his keys and indicated which one to use. They agreed magnanimously that he could start the Eucharist while they took care of the issue.

Ego volo celebrare, he said to himself, *Sanctam Missam,*

et Conficere Corpus et Sanguinem Domini Nostri Iesu Christi, "confect the Eucharist" *the words still surprise me. I am about to prepare a meal of the Body and Blood of Christ. And yet I have to worry about you-know-who in the sacristy. He obviously had no sense of what was about to happen at the altar. Carl probably called it a table. Not because he was some low church Prot but because he didn't know any better. Wish they could have locked him out. What do you do when people are so far from having a faith life? Does Ronny have a faith life? He must, although he gave me his rosary, as in retiring it or giving it better use. Was that because he was "retiring" from Catholicism?* Distracted, he didn't finish the Latin prayer for the right intention to celebrate Mass and started the procession to the altar.

Hacia ti, Morada Santa. The entrance procession song was solemn and long so with the cross bearer, readers and the acolytes Laughlin took the long route to the altar. There was a dramatic aspect to the entrance because only the sanctuary lights were on and the nave was dark. This was so that the candles the acolytes carried would stand out. This was an effect special to the group at Holy Trinity, it seemed. The church was not full; the Neo-Cats were still in a recruiting phase, so a third of the pews in the back were empty. Maybe that was why they liked the dark church.

Most of the back pews were empty, but not the last pew. Two people were standing there. Laughlin was surprised they had not been forced to sit with the rest of the congregation but soon figured out why. There were ushers-enforcers as he called them who strong-armed the people up front. But these were not Neo-Cats in the last pew. They definitely were "visitors," a man and a woman and not Latinos, Laughlin thought, even though he could not make out their faces. Then he could. None other than Mary Horvath and George Kotzebue were standing there in the last pew. *You have got to be kidding me.*

He hissed at them as he walked by. "Get out of here

right now."

Mary Horvath looked at him with surprise.

"Father, we thought we would stay for Mass," she said. George looked very offended by the priest's comment. The acolytes were looked back at Laughlin, who now had stopped.

"Carl is in the sacristy, dressed in his tux pants," the priest said.

"Oh God," said Mary. "What are we going to do?"

"He is going to see you if you don't leave now. I'll call you later. Just leave, ok?"

Please, people, can you be reasonable?

"Ok, we'll go," Mary said.

George looked undecided. *Oh, sure, George, stand your ground now, let's have a meeting right after Mass. Or maybe during the Sign of Peace we could have a little ceremony?*

"Please, he looks almost deranged," said Laughlin and then resumed walking up the aisle.

"Ok, Father, we will wait for your call," said Mary.

Laughlin thought he heard the two walk out, but was not sure until he heard the heavy front doors clang shut.

Pedro and Pablo hadn't locked the front doors yet. They will think I kicked them out. That should make them happy.

As he kissed the altar, Laughlin looked over at the sacristy. He could not see Carl Sand and the sacristy light was out. *Who had turned it off? Usually I do that, but I wouldn't have done that, would I?*

When the first reader went to sit down, Father Laughlin heard a movement in the sacristy. The lights were on again. He tried to look over in that direction discreetly, but the acolytes all turned their heads there too. Carl was looking out at the congregation. *Did he have some crazy clairvoyance and know that he almost caught the two others in the back?*

As he sat down after the collect, Laughlin saw the two Catechists at the back of the church. They were locking the doors. After the first reading the so-called "echo" went very long. That is what the Neo-Cats called their commentary on the Scriptures at Mass. The echo was really not an echo. *A choice, not an echo—who said that? A choice not an echo. Goldwater? Trivial facts have started slipping my memory. I have to police the echo on the second reading, only five people. Most of them come loaded for bear. They already know sometimes what they want to talk about, and find a convenient hook in a phrase from the Bible. And from there on and on.*

The psalm was chanted and Laughlin looked back into the sacristy. Carl had turned the light off but was still looking into the church. *He thinks people cannot see him looking out the door. His head is sticking out the doorway, for crying out loud.*

During the second reading there was a knocking at the back doors of the church. The church was a new building, with a vestibule that was separated from the nave by a glass wall and doors. The outer door of the church was solid with chunks of stained glass. A shadow indicated someone was behind the door. Pedro or Pablo looked at the priest as if to ask whether to go back to the door, but Laughlin shook no. *You were the ones who locked up the joint.*

It was during the Gospel reading that more noise was heard, this time at the side door. Laughlin looked over at Pedro and Pablo. *So much for your bright idea about locking the doors.* He shrugged to tell them to let whoever it was in.

They went out but as he finished the Gospel, he noticed they had come back to the sanctuary and shook their heads as if they did not know what had happened. The echo of the Gospel was very long, although Laughlin hardly said anything for the homily. *The Feast of John the Baptist. I wish I were John the Baptist, I'd be in the desert instead of Zachary, New Jersey, and if they wanted to cut off my head, it would take the pastoral migraines out of my life.*

But the Neo-Cats came up with some thoughts. He cut

off the last three people by pretending not to notice their hands up. Finally, they moved on to the Eucharistic Prayer. Right after the consecration, however, the priest became aware of a stir behind him in the sanctuary, a voice in English and some replies in something similar. When he turned to give the Kiss of Peace, Pedro or Pablo came to him and said, "The man in the sacristy has found a woman fallen on the side steps."

Laughlin looked toward the sacristy and saw Carl standing there. He went over to talk to him during the chaos of the Neo-Cats embracing and kissing each other.

"Priscilla Biden wants to see you," Sand said.

"Bidener. Did you tell her I was in Mass?"

"I told her, but she is in bad shape. She thinks she broke her arm. I tried to have her bend it and she screamed."

"You tried to have her bend a broken arm?"

"She just fell a few steps. I thought maybe it was a pulled muscle or something."

The pulled muscle is in your head!

"Where is she?"

"She is in the vestibule. The doors were locked and she was trying to see in. Then some of the Spanish guys came and opened the door, knocking her down the steps. They must not have seen her, because they closed the doors and went back in. I saw her because I went out for a smoke."

"Did you call 911?"

"Nope, she doesn't want that. She wants to talk to you first."

Laughlin went out through the sacristy to the vestibule.

"Priscilla, what is wrong?"

"I was trying to see what was happening in the church and two men came. They opened the doors so fast I fell. They left me there."

"They didn't see you," Laughlin said. *Per Carl Sand, in defence of Pedro and Pablo.*

"Why were the doors locked if there was a Mass?"

"It was in Spanish, you wouldn't understand."

"They should never lock the doors of the church during services," she said.

"I'm sorry. Do you think you broke your arm? I will call 911. I have to finish Mass."

"No, you can take me to the Emergency Room when you're done."

"I am only half-way through the Mass."

"That's ok."

Laughlin noticed Carl standing behind him. He now was wearing the tux jacket, although still with his tee shirt.

"Carl, could you take Priscilla to the hospital?"

"No way. I could be liable if something happens to her on the way. She could dislocate something. Call the EMS. What if I hurt her getting into the car?"

Hurt her? Like twisting her broken arm? I would like to sue you myself.

"I'm calling 911," Laughlin said.

"I won't go. I'll wait for you," said Priscilla.

"They will probably take just as long as you, anyway. It's a Saturday night and there are lots of emergencies. People bleeding get attention first." said Carl.

"That's real helpful," Laughlin said to him, and he blinked with surprise at the priest's tone.

Now Pedro and Pablo and a few others came into the vestibule.

"I am going back to the Mass," Laughlin said. *I'll try to maintain some dignity.*

"I'll be here, Father," said Priscilla, as if she had all the time in the world.

Chapter Sixteen

A s he shed the vestments in the sacristy, Laughlin was approached by Carl Sand.

"Are you going to pull off the meeting?" he asked.

"What meeting?" asked Laughlin. "I have to go to the hospital with Priscilla and then to a prayer service. There will be no meeting tonight. It'll be eleven o'clock before I get out of there."

"What did you tell Mary?"

"What do you mean, what did I tell Mary?"

Carl got very close to the priest. Laughlin was now standing with his keys in his hand, but practically pinned down against the vestment cases. He noticed the Neo-Cats staring at his exchange with Carl.

"She wanted a meeting tonight."

"She is being as unreasonable as you are."

"So she did ask for a meeting. I knew it."

"How did you know it?"

"Because Joyce Collins told me. At least she had the human decency. She said you were meeting them after Mass. Mary told her that."

"Mary wanted to, but that was before my friend went to the hospital."

"Your friend hasn't gone to the hospital yet; she is waiting in the vestibule."

Sand had an awful smirk when he thought he had

caught someone in a mistake.

"I am not talking about her. My friend Ron is in the hospital. He's here from Trenton."

So important to mention Trenton because it is so pertinent to the discussion. I am an idiot.

"So did you cancel?"

"Cancel what?"

"The meeting with Mary and Devious George?"

Devious George sounds humorous, is he lightening up? What does it refer to, some kind of children's book, why can't I think of the name?

"How do you cancel an appointment you never made? I told them I will see them sometime this week, just as I told you."

"But that doesn't work, Padre. It has to be tonight. Both of us want it tonight."

"Both of you?"

"Me and Mare. She obviously wants to see you, and so do I. Why postpone it?"

"I'm taking an injured woman to the hospital. You have my number call me this week." Laughlin turned to the crowd of Neo-Cats waiting around. "Quien empujó a la senora? Hoy su brazo está quebrada." *My Spanish may not be correct, but my facial expression should tell them I'm angry.*

They hadn't seen the lady. Well, they could go to the vestibule and see her now.

"She thought you knew she had fallen and had done nothing. I accept that you did not know but I am concerned because she thought so. See what locking the doors has done for us? Unintended consequences-- that is why decisions should not be made abruptly."

"But, Padre, you said yes."

"I did and regret that decision," he said, glaring. "You forced me."

They were suitably shocked at his temper.

"Carl, I have to go now. I know you are going through a hard time, but take it easy."

The man is crazy. That stare, it's catatonic. What is he going to do? Maybe he is fantasizing running George over (Devious George whatever that meant) with his car.

"Carl, I want you to go home now. Is there someone there for you?"

"My parents went to the Cape—Martha's Vineyard. They were really pissed because they missed some parties already this year because of the date of the wedding."

The Sands had some dough, go to Florida a month every year, have a beach house in New Jersey but rent a place on Martha's Vineyard for a couple weeks, too. Mary's parents were more Jersey Shore kind of people.

"What about your buddies? The ones you golfed with this morning?"

He is thinking about this.

"I'll call you later," he says.

"Go home," said the priest.

"Yeah," he said.

Laughlin dropped Priscilla at the door of the hospital. She had commented that it was the first time they had driven together in a car. He had a nice car, she said, although she would be glad to straighten it up a little. When was the last time he had vacuumed it?

"Let's take care of your arm, first, ok?" he had said.

He walked her into the Emergency Room to the desk and got her started.

"Hi, Priscilla," said the woman at the desk.

"You know her?" he asked.

"She comes in from time to time. What is it today, Priscilla? Your heart beating too fast again?"

"No, they pushed me down; I fell on the steps on my side. My arm really hurts."

"It was an accident," said Laughlin. "She was on the other side of the door and someone opened it without seeing her and she fell."

"They could have seen me," said Priscilla petulantly.

"I have to park the car. I will be right back. Priscilla, did you call your daughter?"

Why do I always say good-bye and start new business? Must be Jako's influence. I should have asked her about her daughter before mentioning I was going to the car.

"I told her you were taking me to the hospital."

I hope she doesn't want to sue the parish.

"Is there a police report?" asked the woman at the desk.

"There is no need," said Laughlin, "We're going to help. Priscilla is a parishioner."

The woman sighed with a weariness that Laughlin did not like.

"Let me go park, and I will be right back."

His phone went off. He didn't recognize the number.

"Padre, viene? Estamos juntos para el rosario." It was Herlinda.

He had forgotten about the tragedy in Arizona.

"Estoy en el hospital. Una feligresa se cayó en la iglesia."

Will this get me out of it?

"Podemos esperar."

So much for getting out of it.

He took a deep breath and then asked for the address. Where had he put the slip of paper? The house was not far away. If he went he could be back in forty minutes. Maybe

Priscilla would have seen a doctor by then, but he doubted it.

"Where is Rosario? I know where you are saying the rosary. I mean, la Rosario, the one who asked for the prayers. Why are you calling, Herlinda?"

"Because I was the only one with your phone number. Y Rosario está bien *mal.*"

"What is wrong with Rosario?"

"She has migraines," Herlinda said in Spanish. "We gave her Baliums y está descansando."

What did they give her? Baliums. And she's resting. That's Valiums. I hope they didn't give her too much. Hate to have her in a coma. That might complicate things. Who had the Valiums?

"Ya voy."

Under protest, but I am going. Why doesn't any other priest I know have so many complications?

Perhaps because he was so intent on getting to the house to say the rosary—better said to hear the rosary recited by others—he did not notice the white Lexus that was following him. That is, until he pulled into the driveway and was able to see that the Lexus had stopped in the middle of the street.

His phone rang again.

"You don't know me," a woman's voice said.

"Then how about telling me who you are?" Laughlin said. He hoped his anger wasn't too obvious.

"It's about Mary Horvath."

"That is who you are?"

"No, I am a friend of hers. I was supposed to be in her, you know, wedding, but that went to well, you know."

"Who are you?"

"I'm Joyce Collins. I was with Mare one day when she went to see you about the organist."

"You're the maid of honor." *And person of interest in the*

story of Ray Horvath.

"Not exactly, remember it was kinda cancelled. I just wanted to warn you about something."

"Ok."

"Carl, it's about Carl. He's really upset."

I kinda know, sweetheart.

"The whole thing is a terrible trial for everyone."

"Yeah, I mean, but maybe you should know something about Carl. I knew him even before Mare. We kinda, well, I don't want to go into it. I introduced them, anyway. She didn't know about me and him. That doesn't matter; the thing is I wanted you to know…"

"You wanted me to know?"

"Yeah, I thought I could at least tell you. But you wouldn't go to the police, would you? A priest can't do that, can you?"

"What are you talking about Joyce?"

"Ok, I'm going to say it. Carl's got a gun."

He was on the steps of the porch by now.

"A gun? You said a gun?"

The front door opened and somebody said, "Padre!" He was straining to hear Joyce's voice.

"Yeah, and he is violent. Well, not violent, it's just that he has such a bad temper. One time, but I better not tell you about that."

"And you think that he wants to shoot somebody?"

As in George, or Mary or maybe me?

"He's just really upset right now. I wish you would sit down and talk with him."

"It looks like his car is outside the house I am in right now. Oh, no, he has driven off."

The Lexus disappeared down the street.

Laughlin was standing in the doorway. He saw a group of Mexicans sitting in the living room, a picture of Our Lady of Guadalupe propped up on the ledge above the chimney, and several cheap candles burning beside it.

"I am at a wake right now, Joyce. Why don't you try to calm him down? I saw him a bit ago and he said he had talked to you."

"Yeah, but he wants me to invite Mary to my house and she won't come."

"I mean, maybe you could sit and talk to him. He looks really tired. He needs to sleep." *And crazy, mean crazy, like he's thinking about how many bullets are in his gun, which I didn't know about.*

"I invited him to spend the night here. I had to kick my boyfriend out, but Carl doesn't want to, he insists on seeing you at the church."

"Tell him that somebody already called the police on him."

"What?"

"Some of the people at Mass, they saw him and told the pastor about him. The pastor is the police chaplain," said Laughlin

You liar.

"I told you not to get the police involved, Father."

"It wasn't me. Tell him I will call him after I check somebody in the hospital."

Laughlin didn't notice that his voice was getting louder and the Mexicans were looking at him with surprise. They had understood the part about the gun.

"Ha de ser sobre el loco de los tirantes," said one of the men on the couch. Maybe he had been at Mass. Obviously, he had seen Carl's suspenders.

"Father, just be careful, and don't contradict Carl. Do whatever he says, ok? And don't tell him I called you."

"Thank you, Joyce. I have to start the prayers."

Laughlin reached into his pocket for his rosary.

Chapter Seventeen

The prayer was chanted, led by a woman who had come up to New Jersey just to feed and wash the clothes of her four sons who were doing landscaping when not avoiding *la Migra*, but ended up being the official pray-er for family functions. The priest was grateful that they were at the end of the Fourth Mystery when he came in. Laughlin was invited to say a few words to the people around the living room. There were about five women and ten men besides the *rezadora*. The children had been sent to the basement and could be heard screaming their excitement at whatever they were playing down there. He had sneaked a look at his watch and knew that it was about 11 p.m.

"I am very sorry for what happened to your friends, well, your family, in the desert," Laughlin said slowly in Spanish. "That is very sad. I wish I knew how to say something consoling to you, but you have lost family and friends and that is too terrible for words. Let me only say what the Lord Jesus said, 'Blessed are they who mourn, for they shall be comforted.'"

At that moment he saw the shadow on the front window and was curious more than afraid. Who could be there looking in the window? He gestured to the men on the couch who turned around and they saw it, too. Three of them got up and slinked to the back, not without looking out the windows to see if there were other shadows around.

La Migra? Would they really raid a house where people were saying prayers?

He decided to go to the door. *Nobody here but us chickens.*

The house had a small entry way and Laughlin passed through it and opened the screen door quickly.

"What are you doing here?" the priest asked.

"That's what I was going to ask you," said Carl Sand, "I thought you already had a Mass."

"We're saying a rosary for some people who died in the desert. You just scared some of the folks here." *Put that down under "Vain attempt to make the loco feel guilty about stalking me."*

"Are you going back to the parish?"

"Yes, but it is almost eleven o'clock and I cannot see you tonight. Carl, I know what you are going through. But I still have to go to the hospital. I know what you're feeling."

"Oh yeah, is that why you're a priest, some &#% ditched you when you were ready to get hitched."

The Mexicans could hear what he said, even though he was on the porch, and gasped at this. The strange man had used some of the first words they had learned in English.

The dude with attitude knows something about assonance.

"I'm sorry. You're right, I don't know. I meant to say I sympathize because you must feel really like, like," *I can't say fool. Remember he has a gun.* "Like run over by a truck." *Better than shot with a gun, which you don't happen to have on you, Carl Baby? I probably should not have mentioned the bit about running over someone.*

"Worse than that, I feel like someone violated me."

He is still (again) drunk or wouldn't wax romantic--pathetic this way.

"Sure, your manhood." *Excellent, Laughlin, bring that up! You sure have a way with words and they get away from you.* "I mean; you feel like she stabbed you in the back." *He did say "violated" -- stabbed is better than that.* "I mean any man might take it badly at first. But you are bigger than that."

"Who said so?"

"I say so. You are somebody that will find the right woman, and she is not going to get scared or whatever about commitment." *You should have gone over to Joyce Collins's apartment. Oh great, now we are thinking it would be better for him to* whatever *than interrupt rosaries. Well, the rosary was over, but the whole ambience has been thrown off.*

Carl was silent. Laughlin continued to speak, even though he was aware that everyone in the living room was listening.

"This has been the worst day of your life. But God is with you. Maybe He saved you from something worse. Maybe one day you are going to be glad for what happened today because it was something to set you free. God knew you were holding on to something and He pried your fingers open so that He can give you something else."

"That's BS, Father."

"Yeah, you're probably right. I have got to get back to my prayers with these folks, ok? I'll call you tomorrow. Get some sleep. It will restore you. I'm sure you are going to be strong again. God bless you, Carl. I mean it. Good night."

Laughlin turned and went back into the living room. He had just asked the people to forgive the interruption when Carl Sand entered the living room. The eyes of the mourners were wide when they saw him.

"Carl, I said good night, already."

"I have to take a leak, *por favor.*"

Nice touch using the Spanish, Carl.

Laughlin ascertained where the bathroom was next to the kitchen and had someone point Carl to it. The way he was looking around and Laughlin felt that perhaps Carl thought George and Mary were hiding somewhere.

"*Pobrecito,*" he explained to the little congregation, "He was supposed to be married today and his *novia* cancelled ten days ago."

There was a murmured expression of shock.

"Is that why he's carrying the pistol?" asked the man who had stayed on the couch when some of the others had exited.

"He had a pistol?" asked Laughlin.

The man stood up and put his hand, with the index finger extended and the other three pulled back into the seat of his trousers.

"Pistola!" gasped one of the women, and it was hard to tell if she was appalled or just excited.

Laughlin said a few prayers, kneeling in front the image of Our Lady of Guadalupe. He hoped the solemnity of the gesture would make up for the shortness of the prayers. After he had said *Dadles Senor, el Descanso Eterno* prayer three times he stood up.

Herlinda spoke, "Padre, could you give a blessing to Rosario. She is upstairs in the bedroom. She is so *triste*."

Carl was still in the bathroom. Laughlin climbed the stairs with Herlinda. Rosario was fully clothed, lying on a bunch of pillows on the bed. She opened her eyes.

"I am so sorry for what happened," said the priest.

"My poor mother. She laments letting him go. My family will never forgive me."

"Of course you feel terrible. But we have to accept God's plan, no matter how hard it is. The cross. You wanted the best for him. I am so sorry."

He was stammering out a message of consolation in Spanish when he heard someone barrelling up the stairs. It was Carl, who entered the room suddenly.

"Oh," said Carl. He looked oddly chastened.

"This is the lady who lost her brother. He died in the desert in that terrible incident when someone abandoned a group of people."

Laughlin verified that there was a suspicious angle in

the cloth of the back of Carl's tux jacket. They walked down the stairs together and Laughlin considered for a moment grabbing the gun out of Carl's pants. *What if it went off and I gave him a double-wide you-know-what?* He stood at the door as the other went out on the porch.

"See you later, Father," Carl said.

"Tomorrow," said Laughlin.

"Yeah, right" said Carl. But then he left, even saying "Adios" as he walked out the door. And the people responded "Adios" to him.

Suddenly Laughlin, too, felt the call of nature. He followed the path Sand had taken originally and came to the bathroom, which was located adjacent to the kitchen. *Old house.* When he opened the door the foul odor hit him like a slap in the face. *What on earth! What the heck was Carl eating? This is beyond parody.* With reluctance, he closed the door of the small room and did his business. He chuckled at the absurdity of the situation. *"Who had used the bathroom? The amigo of the padre. What do those gavachos eat?"*

He had to control his desire to laugh as he returned to the living room. *Don't anybody go in there right away!* Then he thought, *Now, they'll think it was me!*

"Estás bien, Padre?" asked the rezadora.

"Si, pero que tengo que irme al hospital."

"What is wrong Padre, are you sick?"

That's without even checking out el excusado.

Somewhat laboriously, he told them about Priscilla breaking her arm and about his friend Ron. He forgot that he had mentioned most of this before. They thanked him profusely for coming and wanted him to eat some tacos, but he said he had to go.

They insisted that he take some tacos with him. He acceded, remembering that he had hardly eaten. *The salad at the Tropicana—I should have had a burger, too.* With his two paper plates jammed with pork and chicken tacos and wrapped in aluminium foil, and put in a plastic bag, he took his leave. On the top step of the porch, he noticed the white Lexus was parked down the street.

Then a woman appeared in the doorway of the porch. "Padre," she said.

It was the *rezadora*. Herlinda then appeared behind the woman and spoke up. Would the *padre* mind driving the lady home? She lived near the hospital, and it was late. She had two grandchildren with her. By the time she got her plate of tacos and the children came up from the basement, Laughlin was a bit impatient. The time was 11:17.

Of course, the three had to use the backseat, because she had to sit between the two or they would fight, which meant that he had to shove some books to one side. He had bought some and left them in the car because of forgetfulness. There were also some newspapers in Spanish that someone had given him, from Columbia. It took an extra three minutes for the woman and her two grandsons get in the back.

He got in his car in the driveway and pulled out without turning on his lights. *The advantage of having a cheap car—the lights are not automatic.* He drove by the Lexus and noticed that Carl Sand seemed to be sleeping at the wheel. *Good sign.*

"Sad about the people in the desert," he said to the lady.

"Life is sad, que podemos decir?"

"You're right, what is there to say?" *Can't beat these people in piety.*

"To say? That God help us. Maybe he spared them this crazy life here, where they lose their faith and their morals."

"But to die in the desert?"

"The desert is as close to heaven as we are right now," she said. "God gave them a shortcut while they still had hope for something better."

Talk about Debbie Downer!

"This country will fall down. Like all the empires before it. Sometimes in my dreams I see the skyscrapers of Nueva York fall down, one after the other, like dominoes." *Rezadora y profetisa and international Deborah-downer.*

Meanwhile, the boys asked to begin eating the tacos and of course the woman said yes. *Salsa and taco crumbs in the back seat, great! Now Priscilla will have a lot to clean.* The noise of the grandsons crunching the tacos made him laugh, however. The empire was going down, but we like these fried tacos. The woman was not sure of the street, but one of the boys, probably six, told him where to turn. He got in the driveway of a big old white house that needed some paint. He helped the lady get out, but the boys spilled some tacos on the car seat.

"Gather them up," said the *rezadora*. "The padre's car is clean."

Not so much, but especially not after this.

When he got to Trinitas, Laughlin pulled into the parking lot by Emergency.

As he entered the area of the cubicles, he heard Priscilla Bidener's voice.

"Where is he? He said he was coming back. Maybe something happened to him in the parking lot. Maybe he fell."

Laughlin could hear the voice of the orderly, a man, ask whether the priest had problems with falling.

"No, but neither did I. Or he could have got mugged. This city is not safe."

The priest walked to where Priscilla was lying in a bed.

"Priscilla, how are you doing?"

"What happened?"

"I was called to a house. There was a death in a family and they wanted to talk to me."

"You left me alone."

"No, I left you in good hands. What did the doctor say?"

"Doctor? Like I have seen a doctor. It took them two hours to have me get an X-ray. The doctor is busy. There is man down the hall who was shot. I got here first, but I guess he is bleeding."

"That is very Christian of you to be so patient," he said.

The orderly could not contain a laugh.

"That's enough out of you, young man. You haven't been here for hours."

"I'm sorry, ma'am," the man said, but he was still smiling.

"Did your daughter say she was coming?" Laughlin asked.

"Yeah, she said so, but that was hours ago, too. She probably had to finish her dinner with Fatso."

The orderly, a young African-American started laughing again.

"You think I'm kidding. The guy weighs, I don't know, 350 pounds. That's in the altogether, after the wind blows the dust off of him. My daughter feeds him too much. He's always eating weird things. Quail eggs, for instance, as if there were not enough chickens in New Jersey to supply his hunger for eggs. They're eggs, just little tiny ones. Hardly worth peeling, which he makes her do, anyway. And expensive."

Laughlin wondered how to get off this subject, but was relieved by the arrival of Priscilla's daughter.

"What did you do now, Ma?" she said. "Hi, Father. Don't you get enough of her?"

"Listen to her," said Priscilla. "I broke my arm and she starts joking."

"You broke your arm, really?"

"I told you that on the phone."

"Yeah but I thought you just *thought* you broke your arm. Did the doctor say it?"

"Yes, ma'am. Trying to decide whether to set it with surgery or just a cast." This was the orderly.

Laughlin was surprised at this information.

"Surgery?" he asked. *Of course they had to lock the church and I had to say yes.*

"I don't want surgery. Put it in cast and let me go home."

"We'll do what the doctor ordered. What happened, Ma?"

"I fell on the steps of the church."

"At night?"

"Father was having a Mass and you know how I love to see him say Mass."

"It was a Mass in Spanish, and some of the men had locked the door for security." Laughlin was quite pleased that Priscilla had not talked about being pushed.

"I tried the door and then they opened it and I fell," said Priscilla.

Thank you, Darling.

"You should have been home," said her daughter.

"What would I do at home? I wanted to pray. It's a free country, last I heard."

"When is the doctor coming back?" asked Laughlin.

"Supposingly, in about fifteen minutes," said the orderly. "I was just keeping her company because she was fussing about being alone."

"I think I'm going upstairs to see my friend," said Laughlin, turning to Priscilla's daughter. "A friend of mine from the seminary came up to see me today and his sugar was at 400, he almost passed out at lunch. I had to rush him to the hospital." *Talk about a broken record. My sister would say, 'you want some cheese with that whine?' How did you skip the cancelled wedding and the dying nun?*

"You sure had a busy day," said Priscilla's daughter.

"That's nothing; a wedding was cancelled today," said Priscilla, "The groom was talking to me in the vestibule. He was trying to talk to Father but the Spanish wouldn't let him."

Priscilla's daughter looked at Laughlin to see whether her mother was talking sense.

"Yes, it was for today, but it was cancelled almost two weeks ago. The guy came to church in his tux. It's a mess."

"Oh my God," said Priscilla's daughter.

"Don't take the name of God in vain," said Priscilla.

"I'll be back," said Laughlin.

"What's in the bag?" asked Priscilla.

"Ma, you are so nosey," said her daughter.

"It's a bag of tacos. The Mexicans gave me them. It's my supper."

"You're probably going to get sick," said Priscilla.

He walked out.

Chapter Eighteen

When he got to Ron's room, Laughlin thought that his friend was asleep. He sat down on the chair next to the bed and opened up the tacos. He had forgotten how hungry he was until Priscilla had called attention to what he had been carrying.

Oh good, the crispy tacos. I hope this green sauce is not too hot. Picking up a taco, he let the salsa drip off. He bit into a taco.

"Where have you been?"

"Ronny, you scared me. I was trying to eat this taco."

"And you weren't going to share with a starving man? You know they have not fed me yet."

"Since lunch. You were probably supposed to order something and were asleep."

"Pass me some of them. Homemade by your little *señoritas*!"

Laughlin saw the Ronny was eating them ravenously.

"Take it easy, hombre. Your sugar is all out of whack. That is probably what this IV is about."

"William, tell me something. Why did you bring me here?"

"You were in some kind of blackout. Did you stop taking your insulin?"

"That stuff is expensive, besides the bother of the injections. I have been cutting down on my sugars. I can

158

control it with diet."

"That is not enough. Stress also affects you." Laughlin hesitated. "I called your mother."

"No, you didn't."

"Yes, I did."

"William, you didn't."

"Ronald, I had to. She was worried about you, too. Said she hadn't seen you since they closed the Dry Cleaning down."

"She had to tell you that."

"Well, what happened?"

"The Dry Cleaning is closed temporarily."

"Temporarily?"

"Until I get my rent money together. You would be shocked at how many people leave clothes with me and never return for them. I could have a showroom for Goodwill."

"Your mother said Reginald took some money."

"Oh Momma, you have to say everything, don't you?"

"Well, she was telling me. We are family. Remember how you used to sing the Sly and the Family Stone thing?"

"William, I really don't need to talk about it right now."

"About Reginald?"

"Yes or about the Dry Cleaning."

"When were you going to tell me?"

"Well, if there had been time, I was going to propose something at lunch."

"Which was?"

"You wouldn't go for it."

"Ok."

"What do you mean, ok?"

"I mean if something is that outrageous that you think I am not going to do it, then it has to be outrageously outrageous."

"You are still so coy with words, William."

"So what did Reginald do?"

"I'm not sure, since he disappeared. Maybe he went back to the wilds of Pennsylvania."

"With some of your money?"

"He was going to the bank for me."

"And stole your money?"

"You don't know that. My momma thinks so. But she distrusts all white boys. Present company accepted."

"I think you mean 'excepted.' Who is this guy? I thought you learned your lesson with Floyd."

"Reginald was much nicer than Floyd. That boy was an angry man."

"Why do you let these so-called friends mess you up?"

"It wasn't just friendship. We were business associates. He was working for me because he was homeless. I was mentoring Reginald because I think he has a lot of potential."

"Come on."

"Reginald was a boy from Dubois. Remember how you used to say it, "Doo Bwa?" He is very sincere. There must be some reason for his absence. In fact, I am afraid someone after me got to him."

"Where did you pick him up?"

"I didn't pick him up. He came to apply for a job."

"He was homeless? And of course you hired him? Plus, he had no place to stay, so you let him sleep on the couch in your apartment."

"My momma told you all that?"

"No, I'm just guessing. That's your MO. Find a lost soul, take him home, give him money, and then he vanishes."

"Really, William. You are so insulting. Don't you have any compassion?"

"For gold-diggers? How could you not see through them?"

"Why do you have to accuse me with such a disgusted

look on your face and in that tone of voice?"

"Maybe because I care about you and can't stand seeing you self-destruct with these people who betray you."

There was a knock on the open door of the room. A nurse, a pretty young African-American stood and looked at them in the limited light of the room.

"You're up and you have company!"

"This is my friend or maybe ex-friend William. William, this is Deirdre."

"I don't believe he's an ex-friend. And he brought you some food," she turned toward Laughlin, "He refused to order food because he claimed he was going home. The doctor wouldn't give him permission."

"Deirdre, T.M.I. Ok, let me order something."

"You just ate five tacos," Laughlin said.

"Can you show me the menu, Deirdre dear? William, you are awfully communicative about things that need not be public knowledge."

"Let me take your blood pressure and check your blood first," said Deirdre. "Then you can order."

"I'll be back in a second," said Laughlin, "I want to check if they are going to operate on Priscilla."

"Who's Priscilla?" asked the nurse.

"A *femme fatale* of only eighty odd years," said Ronny.

The nurse was laughing. Ronny was in high style.

Laughlin saw Priscilla's daughter outside of the Emergency Room doors.

"What's up?"

"The doctor is checking one more thing and she probably will go home tonight. I was having a smoke."

"Bad habit," he said.

"I know, but we all have to have some bad habits. I'm really sorry about my mother."

"We are, too. It was a freak accident."

"No, I mean about how she stalks you. I told my sister

Denise, she's in California, and she says I should take Ma's car keys away."

"That would be really tough on her."

"I know, but she's eighty. I know, she wouldn't know what to do with herself. Not that she ever has known what to do. My father treated her like... I better not talk that way with a priest."

"I'm sure she's had a tough life. I'm glad no surgery. Was it her right or left arm?"

"Her left, but she's right-handed. They are just going to try immobilizing it or something. The doctor looks like a kid, like I'd expect him to be asking me if I want fries with that in a McDonald's, and he's the doctor."

"I'm going back to see her."

"Yeah, I need a minute. She tests my patience and I have a habit of getting 'F' on tests of patience."

"You get your humor from your mother."

"I hope that's all I got from her."

"Easy, ok? We make things worse for ourselves sometimes."

"Ain't that the truth?"

"Priscilla?"

"Who is it?"

"Father Laughlin."

"I thought you left."

"I have a friend upstairs."

"I know, Jesus."

"No, in the hospital. Ronald Avery. We went to school together. I told you about him."

"Did he break a limb?"

"I told you, it's sugar. He's got diabetes."

"Ok, so what now?"

"Your daughter says you are going home."

"When will I see you again?"

"You live around the corner from the church."

"I won't be able to drive—according to these dictators. Who said Hitler died and went to heaven?"

Was that supposed to be who died and left you boss? And how did Hitler get dragged in?

"I'll take you communion this week."

"What day?"

"I'll call you."

"Oh yeah, sure. I've heard that one before."

"Well, not from me. I will see you. You better get some sleep; you've had a long day." *Stalking me, hiding in the bushes, trying to break in the church, falling down steps, breaking limbs...*

"Honey, give me a kiss good-bye."

"Sure," said Laughlin, and leaned down to kiss her on her forehead.

"You call that a kiss?"

"What do you want, *Gone with the Wind*? Take it easy, Miss Priscilla."

"Father, I love you."

"I know you do."

"I said I love you."

"And I said, 'I know you do.'"

"That is not the right answer."

"And what is?"

"It's 'I love you, too.'"

"Ok. I love you, too."

"Say it like you mean it."

"Priscilla, I love you."

"You're just saying that." *This is like Ionesco or Beckett, written for Harlequin Romance.*

"Ma, will you stop bothering him?" Her daughter had

shown up. "The doctor says we can go."

"I'll call your mother and see her during the week." *Wait till Jako hears what happened. Two of his favorite things, Priscilla Bidener and the Neo-Cats.*

Ron had finished the tacos when Laughlin came in.

"You ate all the tacos?"

"I was famished. You had promised me lunch before kidnapping me."

"So what did the nurse say about your blood pressure and glucose."

"My sugar has gone down to 350 and my pressure is good."

"Did you order some food?"

"She ordered something 'light'. William, I don't know why I'm here."

"Ronny, you're sick."

"Sick and tired. What do you think is wrong with me?"

"Your diabetes is acting up. Your blood pressure is like a giraffe's. I think you're worn out. You are unlucky in relationships and you trust the wrong people. The business didn't work out. Your family is upset with you. You have painted yourself in a corner."

"Well, Father Freud, aren't you the clever one? The Dry is closed temporarily. I am trying to get a loan from the bank if I can find someone to co-sign."

"We're not allowed to co-sign for loans. Diocesan policy."

"Did I say you? I said 'if I can find someone to co-sign.' I have other friends."

From your lips to God's ears.

"I said, 'I have other friends'," Ronny repeated.

"I heard you."

"How would the bishop even know if you co-signed?"

"Nobody knows what the Shadow knows."

"Don't get racial."

"I'm not. It was a radio show. *The Shadow*."

"I know that. William, a question. Are you happy?"

"What is this about?"

"I mean, are you happy with this life in Small Town, New Jersey, with Father Jacko-Lantern and Fu Manchu and all the crazy people?"

"That's nasty and racial. And put that way, it's not a fair question."

"Why not?"

"Because today has been such a crazy day. I told you about that wedding that was cancelled. Well, Carl, the man whose bride-not-to-be said, 'Forget about it,' is packing a pistol and insisting on a meeting with Mary Horvath, the runaway bride, and her 'friend' George Kotzebue."

"Cots-a-what?"

"He says it's German. Says he's the same name as a famous dramatist."

"Well, sounds like he has some drama on his hands. The aggrieved groom gonna shoot his German ass."

"The aggrieved groom followed me to the rosary tonight. He practically forced his way in because I think he thought I was hiding the two suspects."

"You better watch out, maybe you could be in his sights, too."

"But you would love this; he has to use the bathroom. So the Mexicans show him where it is and he leaves and I'm thinking, he looks a little humble, not his usual MO. The guy is a macho muscle head and he seems almost polite as he tiptoes through the living room. Then I have to go into the bathroom. Remember when Timmy Caine, the guy that dropped out in Fourth Theology because one of the cafeteria girls was pregnant with his baby? He went with us to Niagara Falls and the Shaw Festival? That time he went into the john and it was like mustard gas from the trenches of World War I?"

"William, you really shouldn't remember moments like that," said Ronny, but he had begun to shake with laughter.

"You were the one who followed him in there. It was at that cheap hotel. You came out crying, tears were in your eyes. And you said, 'Tim, is there something wrong?' and he was, like, 'What?'"

"I couldn't help it; the guy must have had something rotten in his gut or evil curse on him. It smelled like death. I don't think even death would smell that bad. He must have been ill."

"His roommate said that was typical. You remember Dick Schuhmeister? He said that he would have to leave when Caine took a dump."

"William, you are making me cry," Ronny was laughing so hard. "I am going to pee in this bed, just stop it. He had a most unfortunate sobriquet that Schuhmeister."

"Unfortunately, true is what you mean."

"I wonder where they are now."

"Where have all the flowers gone? Remember when you sang that? You would sing it at Mass sometimes. Talk about a profanation."

"The Newman Center. It was on the cutting edge."

"Also called the fringe."

"So what is going to happen to your *ménage a trois*?"

"What do you mean?"

"I mean the stink bomber and Mary and whoever the interloper is."

"I suppose we might meet again. But not tonight. I have had enough of them tonight. Midsummer's Night. Carl Sand refused to take Priscilla to the hospital because of liability. Then he arrives with a gun in the back of his trousers at the rosary."

"*Pistola* up the *derriere*?"

"No, shoved into the back of his tux pants. No belt, just elastic waist."

"He was armed and dangerous, especially when he went to that bathroom."

"And the worst thing, Ronny, is that I had to take a pee in there. The next Mexican in there was going to think I was the one who caused the chemical warfare."

"Stop it, I can't take laughing this hard," Ronny said and groaned.

"Hey, guys, what is going on here?" Deirdre had popped her head in.

"I was just telling Ron something that happened to me."

"A tale of the vineyard," said Ronny and then guffawed. "Father Bill is just a humble worker in the vineyard of the Lord."

"My first Mass homily." Now Laughlin was laughing.

"Must be awfully entertaining," Deirdre said. "But it's after eleven-thirty, some of the patients are sleeping."

"Tell him stop bringing up funny things."

Deirdre looked at Laughlin.

"I'm sorry," said the priest. "He must need a laugh, because it wasn't that funny."

"You two are comical," said Deirdre.

When she left, Laughlin said, "When we aren't fighting. Anyway, driving to the hospital with the *rezadora* in the back seat with her two grandsons from Tasmania, she says she has seen Manhattan tumble down, the buildings colliding into each other like dominoes."

"Make a good movie."

"Then Priscilla wanted to kiss me on the lips."

"Who's Priscilla?"

"My *femme fatale*, remember. The old lady the Mexicans pushed down the steps by accident and she broke her arm. She was in the Emergency Room."

"She wanted to kiss you on the lips? And why are the Mexicans pushing love-lorned ladies down the steps? What did you do?"

"I said my lips were for the chalice."

"You did not." Ronny was now shoving a pillow in his face so that his shrieks of laughter would not be heard.

"I know. I kissed her on the forehead."

"A chaste kiss. Father Mac would be proud of you, resisting temptation."

"I assure you, it was not temptation. She's eighty."

"But still young at heart, noticing the hunky priest at Holy Trinity."

"Maybe the hunkiest at Holy Trinity. The competition is less than fierce."

"Don't sell yourself short, William. There were girls at Seton sighing for you. Boys, too, but you never noticed."

"I told your mother we would call her."

"I don't want to talk to her."

"She needs to know what is happening."

"She needs to know nothing."

"At least let me tell her I saw you."

"I will not talk to her."

"Why are you mad at her?"

"Because she gets into my business."

"With Reginald?"

"With everything. She needs to learn a lesson."

Deirdre was back. "Here's the omelette you ordered, Mr. Avery."

"Thank you, Deirdre, but I am losing my appetite thanks to my erstwhile friend here."

"You two sure put on a show. Maybe you should go to the Comedy Club. So should I send the food back?"

"Just set it down here, Child, thank you. I will take care of it."

She giggled.

Laughlin's phone rang again. It was Joyce Collins.

Chapter Nineteen

"Father?"

"Joyce?" Laughlin said as he walked into the hallway.

"Where are you?"

"I am at the hospital visiting my friend. Why are you asking me that?" *Good question and so is: "Why are you telling her?"*

"Because I think Carl is waiting outside the rectory."

"You think?"

"Because he told me that he was waiting for you."

"Outside the rectory?"

"I don't know."

"Joyce, you are way too involved in this thing."

"What do you mean?"

"Why are you taking sides?"

"I am not taking sides. Who told you that, Ray?"

"No. I'm judging that by these phone calls."

Somewhere in the background Laughlin heard a man's voice say some expletives.

Laughlin walked back into Ronny's room.

"Who said that, Joyce?"

"Who said what, Father?"

"Who just said some expletives? I heard a man's voice."

Ronny was suddenly alert. He sat up on the side of the bed and was looking at Laughlin.

"Nobody. I mean. Why are you saying that? Maybe it

was the television."

"Put the phone by the television now."

There was a pause.

"See what I mean? You are with Carl right now. Tell him to calm down. Don't help him be more crazy."

Another silence. Then the phone clicked.

"See what I have to deal with?" Laughlin said, looking at Ronny. "And Jako wants me to take over Holy Trinity? I'd have to be nuts."

"Wait a minute. Jako offered to make you pastor?"

"Not exactly. What he said was he told the bishop that I should be pastor. He's sick. I mean, we knew that, but apparently his doctor called the bishop. He has to retire in two months. I think the bishop mentioned that maybe a Columbian priest could take over because of the Spanish, and Jako said I could do it. He wants a good transition. He does love the parish. He's been there twenty years."

"Sounds like Clinton and Gore."

"What do you mean?"

"A good transition. He wants his vice pastor to move on up."

"I don't know."

"This is good news, William. I'd be willing to move here if you're pastor."

"Let's not be premature." *Do I want him 24-7?*

"Finally, some good news. Then, of course, you will be dean and then you will be chosen bishop. You definitely are bishop material."

"What are you, like, my grandmother or something?"

"I won't be happy until you are a bishop."

"Setting yourself up for a fall. Listen, I'm going home. I need some sleep. This Midsummer's Night is too much for me."

"You're right. Get your rest. We have to plan your installation. I could sing 'Amazing Grace' at communion."

"Not, *If We Only Had Love?*' I might be in a Jacques Brel kind of mood."

"William, could I ask you a really big favour?"

"Sure, you can ask."

I hope we are not back to the co-signing.

"Stay the night with me here. There's another bed in the room."

"I can't stay the night here. What, are you afraid?"

"Then, alright, take me home. I hate hospitals. I can't sleep here."

"They'll let you out tomorrow. You've got an IV in you."

"It's done, look. That bag is flatter than an empty bladder."

"Interesting metaphor. But, just take it easy."

"I want to go home."

"Let me get Deirdre and I'll check if you can."

Maybe she can keep him company until he falls asleep.

"You're not just saying that?"

"Of course, I am saying that. But I don't know what she will say."

"Get her down here. If she says I can go, you take me home."

"Home to Trenton?"

"Home to Holy Trinity. You're going to be the pastor. You can put me up for the night. Come on, William, you're my friend."

"Ok."

He went to the nurses' station. He signalled that he wanted to talk privately with Deirdre. She came over to him.

"What's wrong?"

"He wants to get out, but I don't want to take him home. He needs more attention."

"That's for sure. I'll tell him that. Let's go right now and tell him."

"How about I go and then you tell him that? I have to get out of here," said Laughlin.

"Fine, don't worry. We'll take good care of him, Father."

It was the first time she called him "Father."

"Thanks a million, Deirdre. I am hoping he falls asleep."

"He should, with the way his body is strung out. His pressure is still pretty high."

He walked to the elevator and went down to the first floor. Then he turned to go out through Emergency because his car was parked in the ER lot. He was glad to see that Priscilla was no longer where she had been. He exited the automatic doors and found his car.

When he got to his car he yawned and said, "To bed, *hombre*, you have a big day tomorrow."

Then his cell rang again.

"William?" the voice asked.

"Mother?" Laughlin responded.

"Are you still up?"

No, I'm asleep, I figured out this way to answer the phone in my dreams.

"Yes, I am surprised you still are up."

"It's late here, but I figure you're in a different time zone."

"Ma, I'm in the same time zone as Ohio. New Jersey is east, anyway, and going east usually means it's later than west."

"I can't figure that out."

"Don't worry about it. I'm just coming home from the hospital. I had a crazy day."

"Your sister told me that a wedding got cancelled."

"Can you beat that? The couple went crazy *before* the wedding this time. You know what you say about New Jersey, 'You don't have to be crazy but it would help you understand the people.' Then Ronny is here in the hospital.

Right now I am sneaking out because he wants to come home with me. His sugar and pressure are up. He was incoherent at a restaurant."

"Poor guy. When is he going to be ok?"

"Good question."

"Well, I was just wondering why you hadn't called."

"Ma, I had the Spanish Mass at 8 o'clock, then to the hospital with Priscilla Bidener because she broke her arm when some guys pushed her accidently down the steps, then a rosary for some guys who died in the desert. Plus, some walk-ins that were heavy-duty. Then Ronny." *You're leaving out the offer of the pastorate.*

"You better get some rest, Billy. Those people are going to make you crazy."

"Exactly my reaction, *mater mea.*"

"What, oh, that's Latin isn't it? *Puella est pulchra* is the only thing I remember."

"That's pretty good."

"Ok, get to bed."

"I'll try."

He was by now at the rectory, pulling into the parking garage. He went too far and hit the wall in front of the space. The plasterboard was visibly cracked. Would Jako notice it before he could get it fixed? Why would it have to happen today? He said to himself, but audibly, "Crack up ending to a cracker-jack day," and sighed.

Then he heard a voice behind him saying, "Father Laughlin?"

He was not sure where it was coming from.

"Father, I hope you're not mad at me, I mean us."

The voice sounded so close. Was his phone on? He checked it, but it was not on.

"Father, we are in the back seat," said Mary Horvath.

"Aaah!" he screamed. Then he looked back and saw Mary with George. "You scared me. How did you get in the garage?"

"We've been in the car since the hospital. You were talking on the phone with your mother."

"You heard everything I said?"

"Some of it wasn't clear without context," said George.

Some of it wasn't clear without context. This guy is like a nightmare.

"Why would you hide in my car?"

"Because we saw Carl coming from the parking lot into the lobby. We had asked about where your friend was, but they wouldn't tell us. Then I remembered you drove a Corolla and we figured which one was yours."

"But how did you get in?"

"The passenger doors in the back were not locked."

"I had some Mexican passengers earlier." *But they had my permission.*

"We were avoiding Carl and so we got in. Then we saw that he was walking outside the main entrance so we crouched down in the car. When you left you started talking on the phone and we didn't want to interrupt."

"Ok, we'll go to my office, but it has to be fast."

"What we don't know is how Carl missed you. He was waiting in the lobby."

"I had come in through Emergency."

"We won't talk long," said Mary.

Chapter Twenty

They walked down the corridor that attached the house to the garage. Laughlin wondered when the Filipinos had left and listened carefully for any indication the party was not over, but all was silence in the kitchen and dining room.

He went into his office, which still had a slight odor of Glade mixed with vomit. Immediately, Laughlin went over to the open window to pull the curtains. He would regret later that he had not turned the air conditioning on in the whole office.

"Father, George has to use the bathroom," said Mary.

For crying out loud.

Laughlin gestured towards what he always called the water closet, because it didn't look like there would be a door to a half-bath built into the oak of the room. George looked like he did not understand what he was supposed to do and then the priest went into the restroom and turned on the light.

"You have a bathroom in your office?" Mary Horvath was amazed and apparently impressed with this.

"Yeah, this is really the pastor's office, but Father Jako doesn't like it because he felt exposed here. His office window is on the house's courtyard."

Very important information on Midsummer's Night Nightmare.

Laughlin wanted to get it over. He said, "Mary, this has been too crazy."

"I know, I know. It's just that the pressure got too much for us."

The water closet was not soundproof and so they heard the flush of the toilet. When George came out, he carefully closed the door and admired how it had been almost concealed in the woodwork.

"Interesting construction. Must have been a good carpenter, the way this fits in, almost like for a secret passageway."

"George's father and his grandfather were carpenters," said Mary.

Are we trying to make conversation until dawn?

"You wanted to talk to me."

"Yes, we are very sorry for all the trouble this has caused you," said George.

"Thank you." *But a note would have sufficed.*

"We wanted to explain how all this happened," said Mary, and then she looked at George. He didn't take whatever signal this was meant to be and so she continued.

"I met Carl when I was still drinking weekends. He was a wild guy, lots of fun. He was in great shape."

George winced at this.

"Well, he seemed a nice catch. His family was nicer than him. And my parents had been saying that the clock was ticking, I was twenty-six years old, I had better think about babies. I thought it was a thrill. Then he got real protective."

"Possessive," said George.

"Well, like he was jealous of everybody. A guy who looked at me across the bar, the waiter at a restaurant, my doctor. He wanted to be with me when I got my physical for work."

George closed his eyes in embarrassment at this.

"But Carl was like guys I went to high school with, except that he was richer. He was selling cars, so he always had money. I am active and I liked it when we ran in 10ks and even one marathon down in Camden. His friends were more interesting than him, but I guess it was an infatuation."

And we have to go through all of this right now because?

There was a knock on the office door. Laughlin panicked and gestured for Mary and George to go into the water closet.

"Sorry, but I just came back parking lot. I drive Gloria's friend home. Meet young man there."

Fr. Peter was at the half-open door to Laughlin's office.

"Where is he?"

"I have him in my office. He looks beat up or something."

"I'll go see him."

Maybe it's one of the Salvadorans. They were always getting into fights and then coming to the parish.

"I'll bring him here."

Laughlin suddenly realized the awkwardness of speaking to Father Peter through a door only half open. He opened the door completely. The other priest looked around the office. Had he heard something?

Peter had what Jako called an "Asiatic shuffle" sometimes. Laughlin couldn't help thinking of that when he saw Peter cross the main office space. He looked at his watch. 12:30 a.m. He had to celebrate the 7 a.m. Mass tomorrow, although he would not have to preach because the pastor would be giving the financial report. Maybe he could nap before the 12:30 p.m. Spanish Mass.

Peter's office door was open and he could see only the back of the young man. It wasn't Carl Sand, but it wasn't a Hispanic either. The young man turned his head and Laughlin started.

"Ray, what happened to you?"

"I ran into Carl Sand, but it's my fault, I was following him because of something Joyce said to me."

"You can go to your office now," said Father Peter.

So then went into the office. Mary and George were still in the water closet.

"Ray, you should go to the hospital."

"I'm ok. I have to put some ice on my face. He's a madman. Joyce had to stop him. The two were together. I had seen the Lexus parked at Trinitas, and thought, he is up to no good, and I better see what is going on. Joyce had told me that he had a shotgun and thought he was going to get married to Mary tonight. Mary and George are in some kind of shock. I don't think they figured out that cancelling the wedding means they are going to have to get married."

Laughlin gestured toward where the two were hiding. Ray didn't understand what he was trying to say.

"I mean, my sister is a piece of work, too. She and George have been seeing each other secretly for months. Even before she was formally engaged to Carl, there was this chemistry. Then she is still wearing the engagement ring Carl gave her. Figure that out."

"Your sister is in the next room," said Laughlin.

"The next room?"

"Actually the water closet—er—bathroom. They might as well come out; they're probably listening."

The oak door opened and Mary came out first. George was blushing, Laughlin noticed, but Mary looked like she wanted to cry. When she saw Ray's face, she hurried over to him.

"What are you guys hiding in there for?" Ray said with shock.

"We were afraid it was Carl," said Mary. "What did he do to you?"

"I guess the correct term is he pistol-whipped me. I

went up to him and Joyce in Trinitas's parking lot. I made the great mistake of trying to take his pistol from his pants. I managed to tear the pants on the seam, but he went berserk on me."

I pull the gun out of his pants, he lunges at me on the stairs, and we fall and tumble down to the first floor. The Mexicans then jump on him. Good thing you didn't take that option.

"Oh, Ray, he could have hurt you. I mean, kill you. Why did you do that? What were they doing there?"

"I think they were waiting for Father Bill."

"We saw the car, too, but it was parked in front of the hospital. We escaped through Emergencey and saw Father's car. It was unlocked. How did they know he was there?"

"Father was telling everyone he was going to see a friend in the hospital. He told Carl, he told Joyce that was where he was."

Ok, I'm a transparent kind of guy. So shoot me. Or maybe he will.

"Maybe you should call the police," said George. "We can report the assault on Ray and the threats he has been making. If anything proves that the wedding should not have taken place, his behaviour does."

Strange point to make if you love the girl.

"So, people, why are we here, exactly?" said Laughlin.

"We wanted to talk to you. There are so many things going through my head."

"Through all of our heads. Like, Mare, why did you keep wearing the ring?" Laughlin asked.

"Oh, Father, I don't know. It's pretty, and it represented something I wanted to do."

She was fingering the ring as she spoke. Laughlin knows this must be about something she cared about, but what that was was certainly not obvious.

"You should have taken it off and sent it to him the day

you called the whole damned thing off," Ray says.

"Ray, don't be mad at me. You know I didn't mean to offend you when I said what I did."

"You said it in front of our parents. They have to accept the wedding fiasco like they have to accept me and my smoking weed. Why did you have to bring me in on it?"

"I thought they knew."

"Knew what?"

"Ray, there is no use to this," said George, "We can settle this later. You are right to object, but your parents knew no more than about the weed. Their doubts will die down according to your... what happens."

"What are you guys talking about?" asked Laughlin. *Could George know about the crack and the necklace?*

"You're right; it just was something I reached for when they were all yelling at me. I'm sorry, Ray. You walk around bloodshot and goofy and think no one notices you're getting high. No wonder you had to drop three classes at Rutgers. And Carl told me about you running from the police."

So, Carl told her part of the story.

"I can't believe that you—never mind," said Ray.

"I agree. You know, you could talk about this at a more appropriate time," said Laughlin. "I wish that you would all sleep on this and we could talk about it tomorrow."

"That's if Carl doesn't catch up with you guys," said Ray, "Then we might be meeting in the hospital."

"Actually that might make it easier for me. I have two friends there right now," said Laughlin.

Just a little yoke. But it seems to have silenced them.

"Let's get down to brass tacks."

A Father Jako line if I ever heard one.

"What is going on with you two? Are you going to get married eventually?" Laughlin asked this in a quiet voice. *Maybe they will guess the level of fatigue I am suffering.*

"Yeah, you guys, after all this blizzard of doo doo, isn't

it time to get off the pot? Mare, why aren't you wearing a ring from *him*?" asked Ray.

"That's part of what we wanted to talk about," said Mary.

Then a voice was heard at the window, "Hellloooo!"

They all jumped. Laughlin held out his arm with his hand palm down to tell the rest to keep silence.

"Helloooo, Billy?"

Laughlin gestured to the water closet and the three others filed in. The priest walked over to the window and opened the curtain a bit.

"Ronny! What the hell are you doing here?"

"I told you I didn't want to stay in the hospital. Then you lied to me. You said you would be back and you came here instead."

"I said I would be back, but didn't say when. How did you get them to release you?"

"They didn't. I decided enough was enough and walked out."

"But how did you get here?"

"Someone you know brought me here."

"Someone I know?"

"Carl brought me here. He said he had an appointment with you."

"Hi, Father," Carl said from somewhere behind Ronny. "I brought your friend to you."

"Carl, what are you doing here?"

Above the office, in what was the pastor's suite, footsteps could be heard.

Now we're in the soup. Jako heard this. He'll be coming down.

"Thank you, Carl, I'll meet you at the front door. Ronny, I'll let you in, but we're going to call your mother. I think your brother John will want to talk with you." *John's the enforcer of the family.*

"William, you are not calling my mother at this hour.

Have you no sense of propriety?"

"And you are outside my window at midnight after you checked yourself out of the hospital? That gives the right to talk about proprieties?"

"William, answer the door. I want in."

"Please, Father," said Carl Sand.

So he can pistol-whip me, perhaps? He's scarier when he talks nice.

"Is Joyce with you?" Laughlin asked.

"No," said Sand.

"She's in the car," said Ronny.

So you worked yourself right into this acting company, heh, Ronny?

"I am going to the front door."

He thought of going straight to the door but instead went to the water closet and opened the door.

"We have company. Stay put here. My friend Ron has come from the hospital with Carl and Joyce."

"Don't let him in," said George.

You're quite the idea man, Georgie.

Laughlin made sure he had his key and walked out of the office door, which locked automatically, and into the night. Ron was still in the hospital gown, with his trousers on underneath. Mr. Sand was in full dress tuxedo, shirt and bow tie included.

"Now, Carl, I am going to ask you a big favour. Take Ronny back to the hospital."

"He don't want to go. I'm not forcing anyone."

Wonderful principle. I hope it extends to not making trouble with a priest after midnight about something that has no remedy, i.e., your wedding cancellation. Which I wonder about your acceptance of, because of the fact that I notice you are wearing a tuxedo.

"Ok, Ron, I'll let you stay in my office tonight. Tomorrow you are going back to the hospital or straight to Trenton."

"We'll talk about that tomorrow when you're in a better mood," said Ronny as he walked past Carl to get in the door. Carl pushed the priest to be able to get in.

Your enemies don't let you down, friends do.

"I still want to talk with you and Mary," said Carl.

"Carl, it's too late."

"Ok, you're right. I just thought I was doing a favor for you bringing your friend back."

"Thank you Carl. You tried to help and I appreciate that, especially considering what you have been through. Now, please, go and take Joyce home. I hope everything works out for you."

There are moments when Sand looks autistic.

"Thank you, Carl, you were a life-saver," said Ronald.

'Gentlemen, there's a contribution for you.' It was a phrase an especially boring professor in the seminary used often.

"You're welcome," said Carl.

He sounds almost normal.

Laughlin put the key in the door and opened it narrowly. He squeezed through the opening and expected Ronald to do the same. Instead, Carl pushed the door open and came in first, with Ron following.

"Ok, Carl, thank you for bringing Ron here, although that did not really help him or me. He should be in the hospital. It showed you have heart, however." *Sounds like the grandmother in* A Good Man Is Hard to Find *complimenting the murderer.*

"Not ready to go yet, Padre," said Carl.

The priest could hear the elevator moving. Jako was coming down. This could be just a night raid on the icebox, as he still called the refrigerator. Or it could be that he had heard the excitement.

"Get in my office," Laughlin said to Ronny. Of course Carl entered also.

"Ok, so what are you going to do?"

Footsteps were heard in the outer office.

"Who's that?" asked Ronny.

"Probably Jako," the priest said in a whisper.

"I'm hiding," said Ronny.

He stood up and was walking toward the water closet door.

"No, not there," hissed Laughlin.

"I have to pee," said Ronny and opened the door and went in.

There was silence. Laughlin was waiting for a scream.

"Where are you hiding Mary?" asked Carl.

"Why do you think I am hiding Mary?"

"Because her brother's car is here. Devious George's car is still parked at the hospital."

Of course he recognized it, he had sold George the car.

"Carl, go home. This is much too late."

There was a tap on the door.

"Yes," said Laughlin in a voice he wished was more natural.

His office door opened. Father Jako was standing in the doorway, dressed in a sweatshirt and boxers.

"What the hell is going on?"

"This is Carl Sand," said Laughlin.

"You the one who was supposed to be married today?" Jako asked.

"Yes, and this priest is hiding my intended bride."

"Well, well, nothing like a bit of drama for Saturday night at the parish office," said Jako. "Listen son, you better get moving along. Father Peter noticed some cars parked from his window and has called the police. It would be a shame to get arrested the day you were supposed to get married."

"There was no reason to call the police," said Carl.

He's practically pouting!

"All I'm saying is that they are coming. Father Peter is their chaplain."

Almost the same lie I told! This has made a definite impression on Carl, although who would not be affected by the sight of Jako in his sweatshirt and boxers?

"Why don't we talk tomorrow," said Laughlin.

"Ok, but you're going to give me enough time."

"Carl, I hear sirens," came a voice near the office window.

"Haven't you closed that window since this afternoon?" asked Jako. "For crying out loud it's like the lunatics' intercom."

"Joyce, we're leaving, get to the car," said Carl.

"Thank you, Carl."

"Right this way, pal," said Jako, standing to the side so Sand could leave the office.

Jako walked him to the door. Then he came back to Laughlin's office.

"You have got to be more careful with these nuts," he said, and then turned on his heel.

Laughlin waited until the elevator went up to say, "Ok, you can come out now."

Ray came out first, then Mary, followed by George.

"Where's Ron?" said the priest, still whispering.

"Peeing," said Ray, "He was too nervous to do it in front of us."

Thank God for modesty.

"We heard everything. George was the one who called the police when you went to the front door."

"Do you have any idea of how crazy all of this is?"

Ronny came out of the water closet.

"Well, you almost got us into a fine mess, Ronny. Why would you come here with that madman? Do you see what he did to Ray?"

"He did that?"

"Yes, your pal, Carl. I don't even know what to say to all of you."

"It's all my fault, Padre," said George. "I should have asked Mary to be my wife a long time ago. I knew before Thanksgiving that I wanted to be married to her. I just had some... maybe reluctance is the word, maybe cowardice. It's not exactly like what you might think hearing Ray. But Ray and I have had some long talks. Unfortunately, I shared some of what we talked about with Mary. When she heard about the blackmail, that was the decisive break with Carl.

"I have nothing against Carl personally. Well, now, with the beating he gave Ray, maybe. But the point is I was more against Mary being with him than for her being with me."

So they knew about the necklace.

"You're so smart about other people's issues, you never guessed Mary was waiting for you to ask her?" said Ray.

"Hmm. This is really getting interesting. Better than television," said Ronny.

"Ronny, don't feel obliged to make any comments."

"I didn't feel obliged, just sharing."

"Too much. Sharing too much," said Laughlin.

"Sorry."

"Ray is right. I was afraid that Mary would not want me. I don't have money. My family is pretty dysfunctional. What can I give her?"

"You can give me yourself," said Mary.

"Oh, Mary, you go, girl."

"Ron, please."

"Well, George, your turn," said Ronny.

"Mary, I really want to be with you."

"A little bit more explicit, George," said Ronny.

"I want you to marry me."

"Excellent," said Ronny.

Mary started to weep. "George, I need you."

"Come on, honey, you have to say it, 'I want to marry you, too,'" Ronny said.

"He's right, George," said Mary, "I want to marry you, too."

Ronny started applauding. Then they heard the crash.

Chapter Twenty-One

They had to go to the back of the house to see what had happened. A car had hit the Lexus, tearing off the door that had been open. Carl was lying on the ground. Joyce was standing above him in a posture that suggested hysteria. The car that had hit the Lexus was stopped.

Laughlin ran out to the yard.

"Oh my God, Priscilla, what did you do?"

"I had to get my car. I walked over here from my house and started driving. I forgot my glasses at home and I'm tired and then he opened the door on purpose. I couldn't turn fast enough with this cast on my arm. Are they going to put me in jail?"

"My leg, I think my leg is broken," said Carl.

"I'll call 911," said the priest.

"Wait a minute; I think I can get up."

Carl Sand stood up and shifted his weight awkwardly, fell rather than sat on the front seat of his car and then swore like a demon.

"You should go to the hospital," said Laughlin. "Joyce, why don't you drive?"

"Without a car door?"

"Oh, yeah," said the priest. "Let me call 911."

The police arrived with flashers but no siren. Ronny came out to the parking, which made one of the EMS men do a double-take because of the hospital gown.

Emergencies energize Old Ron.

Priscilla was crying so hard the policeman hugged her, awkwardly, of course, because of the cast on her arm.

"What was the problem here?" he said.

"No problem, officer," Carl said. "An accident."

Sand had seen Ray Horvath come out of the rectory. His victim was standing at a little distance and the policeman had nodded to him.

"You were just in the ER. Did you remember who attacked you?"

"Not yet," said Ray, "I'll let you know."

Carl looks concerned, which is probably good for us.

"Well, what happened?" The policeman was about the same age as Sand.

"I opened the door to get out and then she must not have seen me."

"I just got out of the hospital, officer," said Priscilla, with a definite whine to her voice, "It happened right here. I was trying to get into the church and it was locked and then someone pushed me down the steps."

Now we're back to that.

"So why are you here?"

"Because I left my car here. I have my medicine in it. I needed it."

If she was lying, it was a clever dissembling.

"Ma'am, you should not be out this late. Who brought you here?"

"I walked here," Priscilla said and then began to sob.

"And what were you doing here at this hour?" the policeman asked Carl.

"I had an appointment with the priest."

"After midnight?"

"I was supposed to be married today."

"Yesterday," said Ron, causing the policeman to look at him.

"Are you from the hospital, too?" He was looking at Ron.

"His sugar was too high, I had to take him to Emergency. He should not have left the hospital, but he got a ride from Carl and Joyce here," said the priest.

Very helpful information for all concerned.

Joyce winced when he said this, and Laughlin noticed Ray was staring at her.

"So which was it? An appointment or a ride?"

"It was a little complicated," began Laughlin.

"Yeah, I'd say so. And you have obviously been drinking. Would you take a Breathalyzer test?" He looked at Carl.

"Officer, I'm dying from pain right now," said Carl. His legs were spread out straight from the side of the car. "I think my leg is broken."

The EMS pulled up. *Had George really called the police? Why would the patrol car come here before the EMS?*

Carl almost fainted when the EMS squad came out of the ambulance.

"Over here. My leg, it's on fire with pain. I think I broke it."

Where did the gun go? He must have thrown it to Joyce, because it didn't fall out when they put him on the stretcher, tux and all.

"Is someone going with him to the hospital?" asked the tech.

Ray was looking at Joyce and so did the priest.

"I guess I could," she said, "But how am I going to get home?"

"I'll call someone, babe. Come with me," said Carl.

"Is this the bride-to-be?" asked the policeman.

"No, I was a bridesmaid, supposedly."

Ronny started laughing, which made the policeman look at him.

"Are you alright, sir?"

"Yes, officer, I'm sorry. It's been a long day. A long day's journey into night."

Nice. I'm sure the policeman has read Eugene O'Neill. You could be resting in the hospital.

"I guess I will get the rest from you in the Emergency Room," said the policeman.

"It was an accident. Take care of the old lady," said Carl.

"Now he's worried about the old lady," whispered Priscilla. Ronny started laughing again.

"Officer, could you give this lady a ride home?" asked Ronny.

Why are you getting involved in this?

"Sure, I'll take you home, ma'am. Just get your medicine out of the car."

Priscilla looked like someone caught in a lie.

"Oh, yeah, let me see. Father, help me find the medicine, please."

Laughlin looked in the front seat and did not find any medicine.

"Did you put it in the glove compartment?" he asked her.

"Keep looking, Father. Is it by my purse?"

"Nothing here but a Mr. Donut bag, Priscilla," said Laughlin. The donut didn't look too old.

"That's it," said Priscilla and squeezed the bag into a ball in her hand and held it close to her hip.

"I appreciate this, officer," the priest said to the policeman.

"Crazy night you're having," said the policeman.

Tell me about it, Officer!

Meanwhile Joyce was looking like a zombie as they lifted Carl into the ambulance.

"Ray, could you do me a favor?" she said sweetly.

Ray came up to her and she said, "Give this to your sister, ok?" I don't want to take my purse to the hospital."

"Won't you need your purse?" asked Ray.

"No, I don't. Thank you," she said as she pressed the purse into his hands.

Priscilla and the policeman drove off. Then the ambulance left. The three men left there looked at each other.

"She's got his gun in the purse," said Ray.

Of course. Not good to have that in an Emergency Room.

"Let's call it a night," said the priest.

"Yeah, it's one-thirty already," said Ray. "I'm going to ask Mary if she is going home with me."

George and Mary were on their way out of the house when the others came to the door. *Lucky I don't have a key to the back door. We could have missed each other.*

"What happened?" asked Mary.

"A car hit Carl, and he thinks he broke his leg."

"Oh my God," said Mary.

"Talk about karma. But he was with Joyce and she went with him to the Emergency Room," said Ray.

"What?"

"He called her 'babe', too," said Ray.

"You can compare notes later," said Laughlin. "I have a seven a.m. Mass tomorrow."

"Thank you for everything, Father. You are such a help, so good," Mary said this and started to cry.

"He is so good," said Ronny.

"Save it," said Laughlin.

Mary decided to go home with Ray, and George did not seem so upset about it.

Chapter Twenty-Two

"*Vaya con Dios*," said Ronny as their cars left the parking lot.

"It's *vayan*, plural," said Laughlin.

"You do that just to ruin the moment or what?" asked Ronny. "Well, all's well that ends well. I was impressed with your pastoral care of these people."

"Uh-huh," grunted Laughlin.

When he had made up the couch in his office, Laughlin said to Ronny, "Are you sure that you shouldn't go back to the hospital?"

"And be in the ER with that nut?"

"You mean your chauffeur?"

"I asked for a ride because you didn't come back."

"Good night, Ronny, I'm down for the count. And you know it's only one night. I'm not the pastor."

"Yet, but soon to be. I have a dream."

"Easy, that's confidential. Don't be dreaming too much."

"Midsummer Eve Night's Dream."

"There's no Eve in it."

"You're so picky."

"Just leave me alone. I have had enough of humanity for the moment."

"Hey, all's well that ends well."

Laughlin paused in the lobby. He looked up where the crucifix usually hung and then wondered why he hadn't seen it at the house with the rosary. Where had they put it? He would have to look for it tomorrow. Maybe Herlinda had found some other place for it. He took a deep breath.

All's well that ends well, Ronny says. Always so cultured. What was well about this? It's three o'clock in the morning, the Lexus was just towed away. You're not supposed to be here. This whole thing has been a nightmare.

Laughlin went into the chapel. He decided that he didn't have a taste for Hebrew poetry at this hour, but felt guilty and picked up his breviary. Midday prayer was where the tell-tale ribbon lay. Reading the psalms quickly, he decided that he should pause before charging on Evening Prayer. In the pew ahead was Father Peter's spiritual reading. The priest opened where the priest had a bookmark of the Sacred Heart of Jesus with the *Anima Christi* written on the back.

There was a new section underlined:

> *In the distribution of human life, we find that a great part of it passes away in* evil *doing; a greater part yet in doing* just *nothing at all; and effectually the whole in doing things besides our business.*

"No expletive deleted, Sherlock," he actually said aloud. Then he looked at the tabernacle and remembered that his Opus Dei friends said that every tabernacle had an angel assigned to adore Christ in the sacrament every single minute of every day.

"If you're not too busy, say a few for me. I am too tired," whispered Laughlin to the angel, "I think even you would be after a day like today."

He started Evening Prayer, reading it more than praying it. When he came to the petition, "You called John the Baptist from his mother's womb to prepare the way of your Son," he started to think how he had not called his mother. *She called me, don't you remember the call in the car with the surprise passengers? You are in bad shape, dude.* At least he had talked to her. He closed his eyes. It would be just a second and then he would move on to Night Prayer. *Nunc dimittis.*

Chapter Twenty-Three

II Father Bill, it is now 6:45 a.m. I think you have Mass," said Father Peter after gently nudging the priest's shoulder.

"Huh? I've got to get ready!"

It took him a while to remember why he was still in the chapel.

"It's ok, just celebrate, Pastor is giving his financial report."

Of course, Peter thinks it's a cinch because I don't have to preach.

"I fell asleep," Laughlin said aloud to himself as much as to Father Peter.

"You were very tired with all that craziness yesterday. Police, EMS, what else?"

What else? Ronny was sleeping in my office! He'll sleep late.

The priest then ran upstairs and threw water on his face and combed his hair. He renewed the deodorant under his arms and then decided to change his tee shirt before putting on a new clergyman's. When he got down to the kitchen, it was 6:55 a.m. He went to the sink for a glass of water. Peter was tucking into a bowl of oatmeal in the nook.

"Peter, did you see Ronny Avery walking around?"

"No," said the priest.

"Ok, he might be coming around. I will have breakfast with him later, tell him, I'll take him out."

He ran over to the sacristy, where Jako was already dressed in an alb.

"Here's the morning glory, ready for another day of building up the kingdom, there are a lot of loonies to save." Jako said. The ministers, all retired folks, including the acolytes, laughed.

"Let's get a move on, buddy, you have five minutes before show time. Your public awaits you. This guy is irresistible to ladies on the safe side of seventy." This last brought a laugh from the group in the sacristy.

Father Laughlin tried to concentrate: *Ego volo celebrare...*

CPSIA information can be obtained
at www.ICGtesting.com
Printed in the USA
BVHW072009120319
542486BV00001B/4/P